Dolls

Dolls
& Other Brief Tales of Unusual Occurrences in Ordinary Places

James Goddard

LEAKY BOOT PRESS

Dolls & Other Brief Tales of Unusual Occurrences in Ordinary Places
by James Goddard

Acknowledgments

"Dolls" was first published 2018 in *Le Zaparogue 18*
edited by Seb Doubinsky

"Elements" was first published 2017 in *Silence is White*
edited by Chris Kelso

This book first published in 2019 by
Leaky Boot Press
http://www.leakyboot.com

ISBN: 978-1-909849-73-0

This book is for
Sabine & Tikuli with love
because I promised them

it's also for ...

John Lyle, for painstakingly reading each story, for making
many valid suggestions... and for his wonderful music

Seb Doubinsky and Matt Bialer for encouragement

Ian R MacLeod for friendship and for being an exemplar

Djelloul Marbrook, for the reading pleasure he has given me

John and Patsie, who won't like the book
but they are my friends

Piyush Tiwari, my little brother in Varanasi

Contents

Introduction

Throughout my life I have come across people who claim to have experienced inexplicable things as they have gone about their everyday routines—raising children, working, making a home, taking a holiday. Perhaps they have seen something at the periphery of their vision, which when they turn to look properly isn't there at all, or seen a sudden movement where no movement should be, maybe in a shadow, or in the corner of a room. Perhaps they have heard the voice of a deceased parent or other loved one reminding them of something long forgotten, or heard familiar music or the loud ticking of a clock in the dead of night. You will certainly know people who have had such experiences. Maybe you have even sensed, seen or heard such things yourself.

Should we think of these unusual things as nothing but our imaginations at play, as visual or auditory hallucinations, as dreams—or as something with a deeper meaning that science and rationality can't yet explain? Whatever they are, they are, of course, supernatural phenomena. I mean 'supernatural' in its widest sense, that is... caused by 'some force beyond current scientific understanding or the laws of nature'.

Fiction writers often overlook these small phenomena in favour of the bigger events that have more dramatic impact. They want to cause horror and outrage, they want readers to shudder with fear and run screaming from the room. But we all know the real world isn't like that, don't we? How many of us, I wonder, really believe that demons, ghouls, malevolent spirits and other evil entities exist and are out to get us, no matter how much we love the thrill of reading about them. Quite simply I find the small events much more interesting because they tend to be more believable, more relevant to the lives we lead.

Friends who live in a nearby street have told me about their 'black crawlies'—small black balls they see scuttling around their home, coming and going, doing no harm—but what are they? Other friends have told me about the occasional sound of someone walking in an unused attic room in their home—who is their visitor? The why, the what, the who don't really matter. People accommodate these manifestations, they become part of the fabric of their lives.

Most of the short stories in this book were written in response to accounts of 'minor hauntings' that have come my way. They don't need dark and stormy nights. They don't need creaking country houses surrounded by ominous trees. They are the stories of ordinary people, people like you and me, with ordinary names, in ordinary places. They are the stories of Everyman and Everywoman, who are made a little less ordinary because they have experienced something inexplicable.

James Goddard
Driffield, East Yorkshire
October, 2018

Dolls

Each day, before the sun was high in the sky, and while the morning shadows were still long, Gonzalo set off to go to his orchard. So it was this morning. He said goodbye to his wife, he thanked her for his breakfast, although it was the same every day—fresh orange juice, bread with olive oil and tomato paste, and strong, black coffee—and quietly left their three-room house.

He walked along the straight, main street of the village, with its shuttered bars and shops, the white painted, stucco walls reflecting the morning light and lending an ethereal quality to the street. In the distance he could see the shining blue of the Mediterranean, unchanging, like his wife, his house, his orchard, his village—it was another constant in his life, something that defined him and kept him in this place.

There were few people about because it was early and, as is the way with small villages, he knew everyone he saw.

"Hola," he called out to each of them, "another hot day, I think."

"Sí," they invariably called back, "another hot one." It was almost always hot. Even in the winter, under the relentless sun, and sheltered by the low mountains of the Sierra de Alhamilla, village days could be hot.

Within a few minutes, he reached the edge of the village and came to his plot of land. For seven generations it had been in his family. Gonzalo's father and grandfather had looked after the land before it passed to him; he'd learned how to tend the orange trees and the olive trees, from them. When he was a boy and young man he'd known that one day the task would be his, and now it was work he was proud to do. Selling his oranges, even though they were plentiful in the village, and hand-pressing his olives into oil had provided a modest, but good, life for his wife and son. Often a villager would come to Gonzalo and tell him that his fruit, his oil, were the best, the very best.

"Because of generations of love," he would reply, then he would smile and the villager would smile back, and both would be happy.

Around the orchard was a two metre high, chain-link fence, it was sagging in places and needed tightening up. Gonzalo knew that it wouldn't keep out anyone who was determined to get into his orchard, but the village was an honest place and strangers were seldom seen.

He took a key from his pocket and removed the padlock from the gate, that too needed attention, a coat of black paint at least.

As he walked among the trees, he nodded to each one he passed; it was as if they were old friends, or family even—which to Gonzalo, in a way, they were. He touched their trunks, and looked for signs of disease. His heart sang, knowing that this good place was his, that he'd helped to make it what it was, that his work kept it the way it was. Every day of the week, except Sundays, he came here, to this small realm where he felt like both a God and a king.

He found his folding chair where he had left it the previous afternoon, and moved it to a pool of shade that he knew would keep the sunlight from him for at least an hour. When that hour was up, he would move again. Then he sat. Some might say that sitting idly isn't work, but Gonzalo knew how important his quiet presence was to these trees.

He looked at the hard, dry earth around him—somewhere between drought stricken and desert—it was always like this, except after rain, and appeared to be incapable of bringing forth such goodness as was found in his fruit. He moved his feet across the ground, and saw dust rise, as if it were glad to be liberated for a while—it was like the spirit of the earth rising belatedly to greet the day. He let his eyes follow the labyrinthine branches of his trees as they twisted into the air. Now, this season, was not the time of blossom or of fruit, but of dry leaves that remained soundless until the breeze of late afternoon.

Then, when he was satisfied that all was well with his trees, he allowed his thoughts to turn to his dolls. They were spread among the orange and olive trees, perhaps twenty of them, perhaps thirty. He didn't know their true number, for he had never counted them. As he sat there, Gonzalo remembered when the first doll had appeared.

****

He had been a young man, and his father had recently died, so he was now master of the orchard. He'd arrived one morning, in the way that he still did, and when he stepped through the gate he noticed the doll on the ground, just below the fence. *Thrown there by children*, he thought. He went to it and picked it up. Dressed for first communion, or perhaps a wedding, it was a pretty doll that a young girl loved and would miss. He propped it against the nearest tree, a tree filled with ripening oranges, believing that its owner might see it and ask for its return. Weeks later it was still there, and on the tree, his oranges were shrivelling for lack of rain.

Gonzalo returned home that night, and told his wife that life might be hard for a while, that unless rain came soon, there would be no fruit to sell.

"We must pray," she'd said.

"You know," he said, smiling in a way that was empty of hope, "that you do the praying for this family. My belief is not so great."

His wife sighed. She berated him for his lack of faith and then left the house and went to the church to pray.

"Many wives were there," she'd said to him when she returned, "but few husbands, all of us praying for rain. God knows that you do not believe, and one day He will punish you."

"Perhaps He is punishing me now," Gonzalo replied, "that is why He has stopped the rain."

"That cannot be, for that punishes both of us, it punishes everyone, even those who faithfully worship."

They'd had that conversation many times before, and Gonzalo knew that it would occur many more times during their life together.

Next morning, Gonzalo took a length of tough cord to his orchard, and the first thing he did when he arrived, was to tie it around the doll and dangle her from a branch of the tree, believing that higher up she would be more visible to her owner. He went about his day as he always did, and then sat and waited. He watched his trees, he watched the faultless sky, he watched for clouds, he hoped for rain. When the afternoon breeze came, he noticed the doll twisting and turning and her hair becoming tousled, and it seemed as if she were alive, as if she was partnering the air in a dance to welcome evening.

On his way back through the village, when the time to return home came, when the evening shadows were long, a shopkeeper sweeping the footpath outside his shop called out to him from a cloud of dust.

"Gonzalo, I see you have a doll hanging from your orange tree. What's that for, my friend, could it be a sacrifice to the rain god?"

Gonzalo paused. He thought of telling the shopkeeper about the doll, but decided that there was no reason why he should.

"Could be, could be," he called back, then he smiled at the settling dust, wished the shopkeeper good afternoon, and continued to his home.

At home, Gonzalo's wife grumbled about the price of onions, the price of rice, the price of diapers for their infant son.

"Still not a cloud in the sky," he said to her when she had finished grumbling.

"I'll go to the church and pray again tomorrow," she replied.

"You do that, wife," he said, then he hugged her and kissed her and held her tight.

In the early hours of the morning, the thunder came. It awoke Gonzalo, but not his wife and, thankfully, not their son. Through their bedroom window he saw lightning turn the sky as bright as day, he saw huge shadows appear and instantly disappear, he felt electricity in the air tingle against his skin. A little later, just a minute or two, no more, he heard the sound of heavy rain dropping onto the village as a storm rolled off the sierra and headed towards the sea. He'd seen such storms by day, and as he heard this storm now, noisy, powerful, the clouds would be roiling, moving swiftly, like a flock of huge birds following a familiar migratory route.

"Prayer works, you only have to believe," his wife said at breakfast a few hours later.

"Maybe it does, maybe!" He smiled at her.

As he stepped out of the house to go to his orchard he could smell the earth, he could smell the air. White stucco walls all around had been washed free of dust, the streets looked fresh. Rainwater was beginning to evaporate as the air warmed, fingers of vapour rose above the ground and then were gone. Overhead, the sky was as blue as it always was, early morning shadows were as long as they always were. That was the way things were, the way things were meant to be. Gonzalo could feel that it was going to be a good day, a very good day, now that the rain had come.

On the long, main street, a man called out to him. He was lifting the shutters of the ferretería, they rattled noisily as they rolled upwards, and fractured the morning quiet.

"Your sacrifice worked, Gonzalo."

It was the same shopkeeper who'd called to him the previous afternoon.

"So it seems," Gonzalo replied, then he smiled and walked on.

Days passed as they always did, and then it was Sunday. While the women went to pray and listen, in the church that faced onto the small plaza at the far end of the main street, the men of the village gathered in a nearby bar.

Gonzalo ordered an Estrella and sipped it gratefully, he felt its coolness inside him as he sat and listened to the conversations of those around him. Soon his glass was empty.

"For the rain," a man said as he placed a full glass of beer in front of Gonzalo, and removed the empty glass. Gonzalo thanked him. He was puzzled, but could not bring himself to ask what the man meant. He continued listening to those around him. Occasionally he said something himself, something of little consequence, but the conversation ceased, and faces turned towards him with respectful expressions such as he had never seen before.

"Why do you look at me in that way? I am Gonzalo, you all know me, we have known each other all our lives." He said.

Faces smiled at him, eyes showing slight amusement, the men nudged each other, nodded like the donkeys that used to pull carts along the main street, then returned to their beer and conversation.

"For the rain," another man said, as he bought more Estrella to Gonzalo a while later.

"For the rain!"

"For the rain!"

"For the rain!"

******

On the following Tuesday, Gonzalo saw a man tentatively push open the orchard gate. His eyes not being what they once were, he was unsure who it was, but all the village men were known to him, and he had seen no strange vehicles enter the village along the only road in, or out of the village. He rose from his folding chair and walked towards the man.

"Hola," the man said as he approached.

"Hola, my friend," Gonzalo answered.

They were standing beside the orange tree from which the doll was hanging.

"I am interested in your doll," the man said, as he perfunctorily made the sign of the cross.

"Oh yes, do you know of the child who owns it."

"It has powers, you know—and I do not know who it once belonged to."

"Powers?"

"Powers that must be from God, for it brought us rain."

Gonzalo wanted to push the man from his orchard, and his silly ideas with him. Instead, he laughed.

"This is just an ordinary doll, a child's toy that someone threw onto my land, it has no magical powers."

"Not magical powers," the man replied, "magic is the work of el Diablo, it has miraculous powers, la obra de Dios."

Gonzalo smiled at the man, he almost pitied him, and was sorry that he was delusional.

"The women, your wife, my wife, they prayed to God for rain and rain came."

"No," the man said emphatically, "it was your doll that gave us rain, I, and all the men of the village know that is so."

"I must return to work now," Gonzalo abruptly said, "you will excuse me. Close the gate as you leave." He turned to walk away. Believing in neither the work of the Devil nor of God, in neither magic nor miracles, he knew that the rain had come because the atmospheric conditions were right. He was glad it had come, his fruit was looking healthy, soon he would harvest his oranges.

"Your doll has a halo of light about its head," the man called after him, "at night. I have seen it, I came to look last night, after Juan José told me of it."

Gonzalo pretended not to hear. He was disquieted, but he continued walking away. The notion of a halo of light about the head of a toy doll was even more ridiculous than magic and miracles.

****

At home that evening, after they had eaten their dinner, after they had put their son to bed, Gonzalo told his wife about his encounter with the man.

"I do not believe it," he said, when he had told her everything.

"Madre de Dios, Madre de Dios, Madre de Dios," she said over and over again, "it is the work of the Devil. I must go to the church and pray."

He laughed as she hurried from the house, and he was certain he heard her call out 'don't laugh, you will go to hell', as her hard-soled shoes clattered along the night-time street.

When she returned she was quiet. She kissed his cheek, then made coffee. They sat and talked for a while, about their lives, about their son, and what the future might hold for them. Then they were silent, together, but apart, as each of them chased their own thoughts.

"I'm going to look," he said to her later, when he'd enjoyed a generous measure of Magno, and felt ready to deal with any superstitious nonsense that came his way. "You go to bed, I will be home soon."

There were only feeble shadows on the main street as he walked towards his orchard, and so close to midnight no one was about beneath the dim street lights and the star speckled sky; the moon was waning and gave little light. The air was still, the village was quiet. He could hear the distant sound of an animal howling. Someone had told him that the wolves were returning, but to him the howling sounded like a dog in another village, higher in the mountains.

As he approached the orchard fence, he looked towards the orange tree from which the doll was hanging. He saw a glow where he knew the doll was. When he reached the fence he laced his fingers through the links and stared. He could see the doll's smile clearly in the glow that emanated from her, it was as cherubic and lovely as it was in the light of the sun.

****

In the years that followed, each time the rain stayed away from the village for longer than was thought normal, a group of village men came to Gonzalo.

"It's time for another doll," they would say, and one of them would hand him a doll. Gonzalo would take the doll and nod, knowing what was expected of him.

He never questioned where the dolls came from, that was of no interest to him. Perhaps they had belonged to their daughters, perhaps they were found discarded somewhere, maybe they even bought them some years.

The second doll he placed on the ground near a tree, and when the rain still didn't come the village men returned.

"You know what you must do, you must make a sacrifice of it," they said.

That doll he crucified, reluctantly hammering nails through its limbs as its face continued to smile, feeling each nail bite into his tree as if it were biting into his own flesh. Others,

18

in later years, he garrotted and decapitated and burned until their plastic bodies bubbled. Then he left them prominently displayed in his orchard, a parody of the worst depravity of mankind, offerings to a God he could never acknowledge.

Each year the thunder and lightning and rain came. Each year the white stucco walls of the village were washed clean, each year fingers of water vapour rose from the streets and vanished. Each year the new doll had a head that glowed in the dark of night. And for weeks after each storm, in the bar on Sunday mornings, Gonzalo never wanted for beer.

"For the rain!"
"For the rain!"
"For the rain!"

****

He thought about how long ago that first doll had been, *thirty years, at least.*

His hair was grey now, his wife had filled out, and had taken to wearing shawls that she crocheted herself. Sometimes his joints ached, but not today.

Their son was a grown man, with two children of his own. José lived in the city; he worked with computers and hardly ever returned to the village. Gonzalo worried about who would care for the orchard when he died; he worried about who would love his trees.

There were less people in the village now, and he expected that one day his community would be like so many other villages scattered across the Sierra de Alhamilla, a forgotten place of broken walls and ghosts and dust.

Sometimes tourists drove up the hill to explore. Gonzalo had never known what drew them here. Often they would stop by his orchard and look at his dolls. Usually they spoke in English.

"This is disgusting, whoever heard of executing dolls?"
"It's demeaning to women."
"Only a very sick mind would do this."

He stayed hidden amongst his trees. He heard their words. He didn't know whether they were American or English or

Australian, they were all the same to him. When they walked on he always laughed out loud. Perhaps they heard him laugh. They didn't know that when it came to sacrificing dolls, he simply had no choice.

****

When the afternoon breeze began, Gonzalo gathered his things and set out for home. He nodded to each tree he passed, as if they were old friends, or family even—which to him, in a way, they were. He touched their trunks and said goodbye. He locked his orchard gate, and walked back along the main street, saying ¡buenas tardes to everyone he saw.

As he entered his house, he smiled at his wife. They were almost beyond words now, so many years had they been together.

"Coffee?" Was all she said.

Later, they sat and looked at each other. They both smiled.

"How was your day?" She asked.

"As always," he replied, "just as always."

(For Cristina Macia & Ian Watson)

Radios

When he was a child, each time he visited his grandparents, Robert hugged and kissed his grandmother as he was expected to do, drank the small glass of milk she gave him and ate the two Jaffa Cakes from their pretty little plate. It was a ritual, just as it was a ritual for his mother and grandmother to sit talking about the most boring things—the new blouse his mother was wearing, the operation a neighbour had needed, a dog somewhere that wouldn't stop barking.

Robert grew fidgety, and within ten minutes of arriving his mother would say:

"Go out and see grandad then, I know that's where you want to be."

"You know where he is… where he always is," grandma would add, and both women would laugh for a moment in a way that didn't sound at all happy to Robert.

He would open the kitchen door, step onto the herringbone patterned, brick garden path and carefully close the door behind him. He wanted to run along the path to the shed his grandfather always called his workshop, but his mother had warned him about running, and so he walked quite slowly, letting his right hand trail through whatever flowers and shrubs were at hand height, collecting dewdrops and spider webs in equal measure.

By the time he was within ten feet of grandpa's shed, a gruff voice would call out:

"I know you're a-coming boy, I hear you, get a move on and give your old grandad a kiss."

Robert could always hear the smile in grandad's voice and would always run the last few feet.

A familiar aroma of pipe tobacco and what he later learned was called Old Spice reached his nostrils by the time he was at the open shed door; it was the way grandad always smelled, just as grandma always smelled of lavender and his mother always smelled of... he didn't know what, but flowers... something nice that reminded him of roses.

"Come in boy, come in," grandad said as he beckoned for Robert to go to him. Grandad never called him Robert, he didn't even call him Bobby like his friends at school did, it was always 'boy', just 'boy'.

As grandad hugged him, and kissed his cheek, Robert felt the roughness of two or three day's stubble against his face, and wondered if that was what hugging a hedgehog would feel like. He squirmed, and grandad let go of him.

"Getting too old to hug your old grandad are you, boy?" Grandad chuckled as he spoke, placed the stem of his pipe between his teeth, and drew deeply on it. A moment later he tilted his head back and blew a cloud of aromatic smoke towards the shed's roof.

Robert stared at the smoke, watched it swirl, saw in its haze unicorns and mermaids and strange creatures he didn't know. Then the smoke was gone and all that was left was a tickle in his throat.

He looked around the shed. Nothing ever seemed to change here. At one end of grandad's workbench—his desk as he called it—was a stack of old radio cases. Their innards had long ago been removed, scavenged for grandad's important projects, but the cases kept... just in case. There were small boxes filled with jumbled parts, others overflowing with black and brown knobs, and all kinds of tools. Grandad worked in the centre of the desk, where, from his perch on a high kitchen stool, he soldered and buffed and twiddled and fiddled and muttered to himself as something magical grew beneath his fingers. This was grandad's hobby, he liked to rebuild old radios and get them working again.

"Nearly finished this wireless, boy," he said to Robert, "Soon I'll have it back in its case and it will look as pretty as you please. This one's a Radiola Grand from 1923—that makes it older than me, can you believe that? I've even got a battery for it. We'll give it a listen soon."

Robert watched in silence as grandad reached for parts, reassembled the radio, fixed the valves in the top, refitted the tuning knob and other controls and finally lifted a smart wooden case with a cloth covered grille from the floor by his feet. He attached the wire that carried power from the battery, and then slotted everything into the case right where it belonged.

"Isn't she a beauty, boy, a real piece of furniture, a real work of art."

"She is, grandad, she really is," Robert replied, as grandad's enthusiasm became his own. "She's a real work of art." He wasn't certain what that meant, but at ten years old it seemed alright to echo grandad's words.

Grandad, his dead pipe still between his teeth, took a soft cloth and carefully, lovingly, wiped every trace of dust from the Radiola Grand; he ran his fingers over the sleek wood and gently patted his latest treasure. Then he picked up the cloth again and peered and wiped, wiped and peered, until he was sure that every smear left by his fingers had been removed.

A curtain hung full height across the wall behind grandad. Robert had never been allowed to look there, but he'd caught a peek once, and knew it concealed shelves filled with radios that grandad had healed—"he's the radio doctor" grandma had once said. Soon, he also knew, the Radiola Grand would find its place among them.

"Well give it a listen now, boy, are you ready."

"I'm ready grandad, I'm ready."

Grandad reached out and turned a nob. For a moment Robert heard nothing.

"Just warming up," grandad said, perhaps sensing Robert's disappointment, "valves always need to warm up."

Little by little a hissing sound came from the radio, it grew gradually louder, gradually steadier.

"It's working just fine," grandad said, "now let's find a station." He reached forward again and turned the tuning knob until he heard a human voice. He turned another knob and the volume increased a little.

"... *dead. I repeat, President Harding is dead. He died in the night, with his wife by his side. The cause of his death is not yet known, but foul play is not suspected.*"

Grandad tutted, and turned the tuning knob again.

"*This is WJZ coming to you from New York city…*"

Grandad tutted again and turned the knob some more. Then appeared to lose interest.

"You have to remember, 1923 was very early days for wireless. There wasn't the big choice of music and drama and smart talking that we have today. Sometimes it's difficult to find something for these old wirelesses to pick up. I'll try another day at a different time."

"At least you know it works, grandad," Robert said.

"So I do, so I do," grandad replied as he tousled Robert's hair.

****

On the way home, Robert fiddled with the car radio, jumping from one loud music station to another at the push of a button; he guessed that was the tuning, but he didn't know how it worked. It seemed too easy, and he thought he much preferred the way grandad tuned his old radios, turning carefully, listening, listening, never knowing what you would find.

"Stop playing with the radio," his mother said abruptly, "it's annoying, and I need to concentrate on this traffic."

"It's not a radio, it's a wireless, grandad says," Robert said as he turned the radio off and slumped back in his seat.

****

Over the years that followed, Robert and his mother visited his grandparents every few weeks; the visits became less frequent when he turned sixteen and had to concentrate more on his schoolwork. But still he visited them at least six times a year.

By that time he'd learned as much as his grandfather was

prepared to teach him about the inner workings of old radios, which was not really very much. It was as if grandad was the master of an arcane craft, the knowledge and rituals of which, even at fifteen or sixteen, Robert was not old enough to be inducted into. Even when he was at an age when most teenage boys were self-centred and truculent, he was happy to stand beside grandad's workbench and watch him demonstrate, hear him enthuse, and listen to the crackling and hissing snippets of old radio shows that made the old man so happy.

By the time he was nineteen, it was university, and away from home he saw neither his mother nor his grandparents until it was holiday time. He took to calling grandad on a weekly basis, asked him about his latest project, listened as the old man rambled on about things he didn't really understand. His mother he called as little as possible, because she nagged too much.

"Are you eating properly."

"Don't forget to visit the dentist."

"Don't do any dangerous drugs."

"Which ones are dangerous, mum?"

"You know that better than I do, don't do them."

"Don't have unprotected sex with any girl. You're too young to be a father."

"I told you mum, I'm gay."

"You're not gay, you know you're not, I know you're not."

"I never used to be gay, but I decided to change."

"That's silly."

"Remember to eat properly."

"Change your bed sheets."

"Call me again soon."

"Call me again soon."

"Call me again soon."

"I love you, ma."

He couldn't take that very often.

****

When he'd finished his law degree, and finished his in-house placement, he went to work for a city law firm in a junior position. At his level it was dull work, but he hoped to advance. He still conscientiously called grandad every week, but didn't get to see him more than four times a year. He conscientiously called his mother once a week as well; her nagging had changed from that of the worried mother, to that of the neglected mother. She tried to make him feel guilty for not visiting her often enough.

"I have my own life now ma. That's the way it's always been—kids leave home, parents grow older, and sooner or later a new generation might come along."

He almost heard his mother's ears prick up.

"You mean I'm going to be a grandma... why, that's so wonderful Bobby! Why didn't you tell me before now?"

"Don't call me Bobby... and no, you're not going to be a grandma, not yet anyway."

"Well, don't leave it too late. You're not still gay, are you? A man should father children when he's in his prime you know."

"What does that mean? I'm twenty-six, ma."

"Come visit me."

"Come visit me."

"I love you, ma."

He couldn't take that very often either.

****

On the last occasion that he visited his grandad, Robert couldn't help but feel that he'd never see the old man again. He had become very frail, his voice was feeble and his skin was almost transparent and rustled like tissue paper as his fingers moved. They had a conversation of sorts, and Robert learned that grandad hadn't worked on his wirelesses for almost a year.

"You always liked my wirelesses, didn't you boy? You used to stand and watch me for hours, asked me all kinds of questions as you grew older."

"I did, grandad. It was wonderful how you got all those old things working again."

"Well, I'll be dead soon enough, boy, I know it and you know it, and your mother and grandma know it too."

"No, grandad, don't say that," Robert said, knowing the old man was right. He felt tears grow in his eyes, but blinked them back.

"It's true, boy, it's the way things are.

"Don't spend too long with grandad, Bobby, let him sleep." It was his mother's voice, speaking from the door.

"Don't call me Bobby," he muttered, but she was gone.

"I want you to be here for a long time, grandad. A long time." He felt like a small boy saying grandad, but grandad he had always been and grandad he would always be.

"That can't be, boy. But when I die you will have my wirelesses, it's in my will. Your grandma doesn't want them anyway, 'silly old things, for a silly old thing' she says."

"Thank you grandad," Robert said, "thank you." Even as he spoke he wondered where he was going to put forty or fifty old wirelesses in his tiny city apartment.

"One more thing. I built a special wireless for you, Bobby... Robert, whatever your name really is, boy. All my own work it is, using parts from other wirelesses of course."

Hearing his name—both the Bobby he hated, and the Robert he insisted on—coming from those thin lips, Robert almost wept. Grandad had never called him by his name before. It was spoken in an almost admonishing way, as if grandad needed to be listened to because he was aware that his time for words was almost over; but to Robert, hearing his name whispered by that man he knew so well in his workshop, and so little anywhere else, was a moment of true warmth that he had never experienced with grandad before.

At that moment he knew, he knew for certain that he would never see his grandfather alive again.

****

About eight weeks later Robert received a frantic telephone call from his mother. She was sobbing loudly and, afterwards, he was sure the sobbing was more for effect than anything else.

"You must come home. I need you here with me, Bobby."

Don't call me Bobby, my name's Robert, he thought, not bothering to waste his breath saying the words aloud to her.

"Why do you need me there, ma?"

"Because your grandfather died an hour ago and I just need you with me."

He'd been expecting such a call for a while now.

"I'll come as soon as I can, ma, but it will be a couple of days because I have to arrange things here at work."

"I need you now, Bobby, now... come as quickly as you can... for me... please."

He said goodbye to his mother and disconnected his cellphone.

He managed to arrange to finish work that afternoon, a week's compassionate leave was normal in such circumstances, one of the junior partners told him.

On the drive to his old home, he tried to understand why his mother had pretended to be so distraught. It was his paternal grandfather who had passed away, not her own father, as both her parents had died in a car crash years ago, along with his dad. Robert had been a baby when the accident happened and he didn't remember any of them; to him they were little more than smiling faces in family photographs and his mother's occasional reminiscences as he was growing up. He knew she was very fond of his grandma, but he could not remember her ever having offered more than a polite hello and a perfunctory peck on the cheek to grandad.

He decided that her show of grief and anguish was just a pretext to persuade him to visit, but he held his anger in check as he realised that he would have visited for the funeral anyway.

****

He returned to the city the day following his grandad's funeral.

It had been a non-religious ceremony in the crematorium chapel, and Robert had delivered a eulogy in which he mostly spoke about his grandfather's love of old radios. He could see from the expressions on the faces of those who attended that many thought his words were irrelevant, inapt even. But they were not irrelevant to him, and that's all that mattered. He managed to make clear, to himself at least, a deep affection for the tough-bearded old man that he had never been allowed to show when grandad was alive.

At his grandma's house a little later, while the few who had bothered to come were eating polite sandwiches and drinking polite Tio Pepe fino, grandma called him to a quiet corner and spoke to him in a voice that was tired from her grief.

"Robert," she said, "the radios, his radios, he wanted you to have them, he really did. He said I must give them to you, that you are the only one who understands. Please take them with you when you go back to the city. I don't want the things anyway, they will remind me too much of the time we should have spent together, but didn't."

Robert thought he understood what grandma meant; grandad had been obsessed with his radios—his wirelesses.

"I'll take them, grandma, of course I will," he said.

Tears were running down grandma's cheeks, and Robert took her in his arms and hugged her.

"I'll miss him, Robert," her voice was broken by sobs, she trembled. "I'll really miss the crotchety old devil. I'll miss him so much."

After he'd said a hasty goodbye to his mother the following morning, ignoring her pleas for him to say a little longer, and feeling guilty for having done so, he drove to grandma's house. He went to grandad's shed and drew aside the curtain that concealed the shelves with the prized collection of ancient radios. Then he carried them two at a time and packed them carefully into his car—in the boot, on the rear seat, on the floor. He lost track of how many there were at fifty-three or fifty-four. Finally, he came to the one that was packed in a sealed box. It had an envelope on its top, with the word Robert in grandad's shaky hand.

"That's the special one he made for you, Robert," grandma said as he carried the box through the house and to the road outside where he'd parked. "He told me all about that one so many times. It's special."

He said goodbye to grandma, hugged her again. Her tears

were gone after the emotion of the funeral, but he thought they would return again and again as she came to terms with her loneliness.

****

Robert had taken the wirelesses from his car into his small apartment. Most of them were in cases made of Bakelite or wood, he noticed. He placed them on every available surface, around the edges of his living room and even in his bedroom; the one in a box, the special one, he placed on an old newspaper he'd opened on his dining table.

He chose one of the wirelesses at random, plugged it into a power outlet, turned it on, and while it warmed up went to his refrigerator and got a can of chilled beer. By the time he returned to his living room, the cracking and hissing music of the radio was almost lost in the sound of the Glenn Miller Orchestra playing 'American Patrol'—music that even at his age he'd heard often enough to recognise. He looked at the hanging tag grandad had fixed to the radio's speaker grille: *Astor / Mickey KM / 1947*, the label read. Next he tried a model shaped like a church window, he read the label as he sipped his beer and listened to an ancient news broadcast, apparently it was a Philco 90 from nineteen thirty-one. By the time he'd finished his beer he'd tried a dozen of the wirelesses, and heard snatches of programmes that hadn't been broadcast since long before he was born: *The $64,000 Question, Bulldog Drummond, The Jack Benny Program, Abbott and Costello, The Goon Show, The Men From the Ministry* and many more music and light entertainment shows from America and Britain.

He had also begun to wonder about grandad.

What power had the old man possessed to be able to fix up old wirelesses so that they received only broadcasts from years ago and only from the country where the wirelesses was manufactured? How was that even possible? He knew it wasn't possible, he knew… Where did the broadcasts come from after all the years that had passed? Seventy years and more in some cases. How had grandad learned to do this—

where had he learned to do it? These were questions Robert couldn't answer, but for now they intrigued him rather than worried him.

Ignoring his unanswered questions for now, he at last he turned to the special wireless. He carefully peeled the envelope from the top of the box, then removed the machine inside. It was an ugly beast without a case, just the bare innards of valves and transformer and a speaker and other parts he didn't even recognise. Robert felt disappointed, far from being special, it looked to him as if the wireless grandad had made, his special wireless, was incomplete.

Disconsolate, he sat down and opened the envelope. He pulled out the single sheet of folded paper that was inside—a note from grandad, it was short but far from to the point. It explained nothing.

Robert,
Don't listen to this wireless until you understand about the others.
This one is special. When you are ready, just plug it in and turn
it on. Don't adjust anything, I've already tuned it in for you.
Grandad

He slumped back in his chair. He wanted to understand— but what was he supposed to understand? He also wanted another beer, and that was easier to deal with.

On his way back from the kitchen, Robert stopped and plugged in grandad's special wireless. He turned the power knob to the 'on' position as instructed, then he dropped back into his chair and listened to the crackle and hiss that sounded no different to that from any other wireless here.

His beer can opened with a hiss that mingled with that from the wireless, a mist of tiny, cold droplets fell onto his hand. Still the wireless crackled and hissed. He sipped his beer and let his mind wander.

He wasn't sure if he wanted all this old junk. Grandad obviously wanted him to have his wirelesses, but what good were they? He had no interest in them as objects, not really, no matter how much they had fascinated him when he was a child.

He had even less interest in old radio shows. Maybe they had some value on the collectors' market, maybe grandad knew that and wanted him to sell them and benefit from them that way. Maybe... Maybe... Maybe... So many maybes!

Robert was so lost in his thoughts that he wasn't sure for how long he had heard a voice speaking his name. When it registered it send a spine-tingling sensation up and down his back, and he shivered. So softly spoken was the voice that it was almost lost in the ambient noise of his apartment and the mental noise of his thoughts. He concentrated, then got up from his chair and crossed the room to grandad's special wireless. He lowered his head and listened closely, then turned the power knob, that doubled as a volume control on most of these old wirelesses, until he could hear the voice more clearly.

Crackle and hiss still came from the speaker, but there among them was grandad's voice.

Robert stepped back, felt his beer can slip through his fingers and clatter fizzingly onto the wood laminate floor. He reached out to turn the wireless off, but then stopped himself. He looked down at the pool of beer around his feet. Electricity and water. But this wasn't water, it was beer, and he was wearing shoes.

He reached for the power knob again. He didn't want to hear this, and yet he did want to hear it too. He pulled his hand back again.

"Robert, Robert, Robert..." the wireless repeated every few seconds.

"Grandad," he said before he knew why he said it, "is that you?"

Hiss. Crackle. Hiss.

"It's me, boy," grandad's voice said, "it's me. Who else did you think it would be, boy?"

"I don't... I didn't..." He was confused. He was way outside his comfort zone. He knew, though, that it really was his grandad. No one else had ever called him boy.

"I built this special wireless so that I could talk to you. We never really talked much when I was..." grandad's voice faltered, then continued, "... when I was there. Sit down, boy. I have things to tell you."

Robert returned to his chair.

"You think I'm some kind of magician or wizard, that I worked magic on my wirelesses, boy, but I'm not…"

Robert listened. He listened to his grandad talk in a way he had never talked before. He listened. He listened, but he wasn't sure he understood.

Lavender

As Alan climbed into the old car he'd inherited from his father, the first thing he noticed was the smell of worn leather and lavender. He remembered his father once telling him that a few sprigs of dried lavender hanging from his rear-view mirror was better than all the air freshening products on sale at the local automart.

Now, five months after his father had died, he was surprised that the car still smelled of lavender. It was a reminder of his father, one thing he had forgotten among so many lost memories. He reached out and touched the lavender, it rustled like tissue paper as its aroma increased. Touching the past in this small way comforted him, as he had been dreading driving the vehicle to the used car place to see if it was worth anything—or was fit only for the scrap yard.

He reversed the car out of the garage attached to his father's house, and onto the quiet street. Gaping like an open mouth, the garage now looked big and empty, even though his dad's tools were neatly arrayed on hooks around the walls, and the lawnmower was in a far corner beside a set of well organised shelves.

His dad had been a neat man, who liked everything in its appointed place, the front-garden lawn to be trimmed just so, the hedge topiary square, the rear garden full of seasonal vegetables.

"He's a dependable man," Alan's mother had often said.

Recalling that now, Alan wondered if that was her way of saying the she loved her husband. He didn't know, but he felt that if that was all his dad was remembered for, it at least told the world that he was a good man.

His mother had died first. One morning his dad had awoken to find her cold and dead beside him. He'd called Alan in a tearful panic.

"I haven't been alone for sixty years," he said, "I don't know what to do."

Alan rushed home from his work in Barcelona, arranged the funeral, comforted his father, organised domestic help for him for a few hours a week, and returned to his work a fortnight later. When he left, he had the feeling that his dad would soon follow his mother to wherever they'd agreed to meet. Four months later, another call, another funeral, but only himself to comfort. Then he had a house, a home, a life to dispose of. He left that as long as he could.

"But here I am," he thought, as he drove the car along the street towards the main road.

Every time he applied the brakes, gently, to slow a little, an inner voice said 'carefully, carefully, well driven and well maintained, a car will last a lifetime', he knew they were his dad's words. And so it had been with his dad, from the time he could afford a car, he had owned and driven only this one.

Alan had grown up with this car, and it had carried him along all the byways of his life until he was old enough to leave home. Memories were creeping back. Him with his father, him with both his parents, driving off on some important, well planned mission. Holidays by the sea, country picnics, Sunday afternoon fishing, this old car had been a part of all of them. He remembered they had been happy times. He couldn't remember his parents ever fighting, or either one of them shouting or slamming doors. It seemed, too, that skies had been always blue and the sun was always shining—but he knew that wasn't possible.

'Remember to indicate,' the inner voice said as Alan stopped at a road junction. He flipped the indicator on obediently, and waited. 'You can go now, it's clear,' and so he moved onto the main road that would take him to the edge of town where the used car places were.

He didn't know why he was remembering his father's instructions. They were from when he had learned to drive, these words from a dependable man that had always served him well. He wasn't an over-cautious driver like his dad, but he was always aware that he was responsible for his own life as well as the lives of other road users.

Within two or three minutes he entered the band of factories, distribution depots and retail parks that circled the town like a throttling hand. He despised this ugly agglomeration of temples to mammon that had been allowed to spring up, but he knew it served a purpose. He took a left onto an industrial estate road, the buildings he passed were old and shabby, and he guessed they had been built even before he was born. He passed the ice-cream factory, the wine warehouse, the scrap yard, then he drove onto the forecourt of Harry's Used Cars—Always a Bargain—Always a Fair Price. He got out of his dad's old car, and breathed deeply of air that was slightly acrid. 'I understand why you loved the lavender, dad, I really do,' he thought. 'Didn't I always tell you so?' the inner voice replied.

Alan strolled among the ranks of gleaming cars. There must have been almost one-hundred of them glinting in the sunlight, bouncing heat onto anyone who drew near. They weren't the kind of cars anyone wanted to purchase, but more what those who couldn't afford anything better might be attracted to. Among them, he was sure, apart from its age, his dad's car would not look out of place.

A man approached him from a temporary office that looked as if it had been a temporary office for the last forty years.

"See anything you like, mate?" The man asked jauntily.

"I'm not buying," Alan replied, "I'm hoping to sell. Are you Harry?"

"Hahaha," the man laughed without any humour, "there never was a Harry."

"It's over here," Alan wanted to get this over with as soon as possible.

"That old thing," the man said as they crossed to where Alan had parked, "no one will want to buy that."

"It was my dad's car, he loved it, he took care of it until he died."

"That's history no one will care about, mate. Sorry. It's not old enough to be interesting, and it's too old to sell." He shrugged. "That's life. The scrap yard is just down the road."

"The scrap yard it is then," the sadness Alan felt as he said the words almost overflowed as tears. He hadn't realised how he felt about the car. Memories deep and dormant inside him had started to blossom like desert plants showered with rain.

Things he had forgotten, moments in his life, had been creeping back to him ever since he'd climbed into his dad's car for the first time in… in what, twenty years at least.

He began to wonder where those twenty years had gone, why he had drifted so far from his parents and the happy childhood he was now remembering. There had been painful times, for him at least, as he rebelled in the way that all children approaching adulthood do, but his childhood had been happy… it had been happy, and if he was honest with himself, he had to admit that his teenage years had been happy too.

Taking one last look around him, Alan climbed back into the car that was old, but not old enough. He started the engine, drove onto the road and slowly towards the scrap yard. 'I'm glad you didn't leave me there,' the inner voice said.

Lavender, he could smell the lavender so strongly now, it was if he'd rubbed to sprig hanging from the rear-view mirror again.

He reached the scrap yard, pulled in at the side of the road. He stared across at the rusting heaps of twisted, broken metal. Almost all of it had been cars—once, a few unbroken headlamps still managed to glint sorrowfully in the sunlight, chromium plated door handles shone like silver. They were cars like his father's car. Ordinary, everyday cars for dependable people who lived dependable lives, people who were mostly happy in their own small ways, people who created happy memories.

Alan depressed the clutch pedal, reached out and shifted to first gear. He released the hand-brake, depressed the accelerator and moved away from the roadside.

"I won't sell you, I won't dump you. I can't." He said aloud. The smell of lavender grew until it filled the car, and Alan smiled as he drove back to his father's house.

Raggedy-Man

Almost every summer morning on my way to work, and every evening, after I leave my office, I walk through the area of woodland that lies between the edge of town and the modern housing development where I'd bought a house. I work for a logistics company, and it's about a five-minute walk to the woods and another fifteen minutes passing through them.

In the mornings, it was a quiet, solitary time, although sometimes a young paperboy came speeding through the trees, bouncing around on the uneven ground and ringing his bicycle bell, as he rushed to make his deliveries before school began for the day. The woodland floor of moss and grass was resilient, and he left no sign of his passing.

In the evenings, I saw families, mother, father and kids on their early evening walks, holding hands, chattering and, now and then, excitedly pointing things out to each other. Always we nodded, in that slightly distant manner that seems to have replaced actually saying 'good morning' or 'good evening', smiled and went on our different ways—the days on which we stopped to speak for a moment were always a red-letter day.

As the summer wore away towards autumn, as the evenings became a little less bright and the woods a little gloomier, I saw fewer people on my walk home, and the day eventually came when I saw no one at all. That didn't bother me, I liked the growing silence as birds settled down, and often the only thing I heard was the blare of a car horn frantically making a point as it passed along the nearby road.

I grew so familiar with that walk, in both directions, that I had no need to watch where I was going. My feet knew every inch of the route—where there were dips that might cause a stumble, where there were raised tree roots over which I might trip. Even in the autumn, when I could see stars appearing in the darkening sky, and the woods were almost as dark as night, I continued to walk home through that familiar place. If I should need light, there was always the torch built into my smartphone.

Thinking back now, it must have been early October when I felt that I was being followed on my walk home. I didn't hear anything, it was more the kind of feeling that we all get from time to time, that there is someone close, someone looking over our shoulder, yet when we look there is no one there. I glanced behind me, then stopped and turned. Of course, in the dark I could see nothing but the outlines of trees.

Taking my phone from the breast pocket of my jacket, I flicked to torch mode and shone the bright light around. At first, I could see nothing unusual, just trees and shadows, but as I turned towards home again, the beam of the torch passed across something. I saw it for only a moment, and then it withdrew into itself and, like a wisp of smoke, was gone.

Will-o-the-wisp was the first thought that came to mind, but I instantly knew that wasn't possible among these trees, especially with no marshy ground nearby.

I shone the torch around again. The effect of the light glancing across tree trunks, reminded me of a movie juddering in one of the old-fashioned projectors. You don't get that nowadays with everything being digital. The light hit nothing untoward, of course, so I shrugged off what I thought I'd seen as imagination, put my phone away, and continued walking home.

Petronella and I had separated after twelve years together. We'd never married and there were no kids. After a lot of good times, we'd just decided that we both needed a change, to go in different directions. That's when I bought the house here. As nice as the house was, I still felt sad returning each day to a home with no love, no human warmth in it. I hoped that would change for the better one day.

Next morning, I set off for work at about eight o'clock, as usual. The street was quiet. It was a fine, bright morning, with autumn sunshine casting long shadows that looked as if they were trying to pull free from whatever cast them. Reaching the road that was the boundary between the housing development and the woods, I waited for a break in what passed for rush-hour traffic here and then crossed.

"You saw it, I know you saw it."

I was no more than five or six paces into the trees when I heard the voice. I must be honest, and say that the voice made me jump much more than is reasonable in a rational adult. My mind hadn't really been on my route, but had been off doing something of its own and, anyway, I was accustomed to seeing only the ting-a-ling paperboy in the mornings.

"I know you saw it, I said."

Then I saw a man walking parallel to me, just a few feet away. I glanced at him. He was quite old, and if he became threatening I knew I'd be able to take care of myself. From the way he was dressed, it was obvious that he was a tramp, a gentleman of the road, a hobo. String around his middle held a tattered heavy overcoat—ex-military I guessed—closed around him, it fell almost to his ankles, where it met a broken and worn-out pair of Doc Martens. Beneath the coat, he could have been stark naked for all I could tell. The battered trilby hat on his head was so covered with filth that it was a wonder he was still alive.

"I know you saw it, I said," he said again.

"Saw what?" I asked, deciding to play his game.

"It—you know—it. That thing. Last night."

I hadn't thought about 'it' at all this morning, until now.

"It vanished. It always does that."

"You've seen it before?" I asked.

"Every evening. Just like I see you every evening—and every morning too. And that noisy kid on his bike."

This disconcerted me, because I'd never seen the man before.

"Do you live in these woods?" I asked him.

Then I realised he was no longer there. In a few seconds,

he'd vanished, gone off on whatever errand seemed important to a man like him.

As I continued walking to work, I wondered if he was the cause of me thinking I was being followed last night, that I really was being followed. I caught sight of him a few times, or, rather, I caught sight of his shadow, flitting in and out among the trees.

Thinking about this man brought back memories from my childhood. There seemed to be more tramps in those days. I remember how my friends and I, if we saw a tramp, used to taunt him. As is the way with boys of a certain age, a cruel chant or rhyme always seems to come along when they need one, and so one came to us. I can't remember which of us started chanting when we saw our first tramp, I don't think it was me, but it could have been Bobby or Frank or Mervyn, or even the baby of our band, Sam. Whoever it was, just began chanting in a sing-song voice, and within a few seconds we were all chanting the same words, it was as if they'd bounced from mind to mind.

Raggedy-man, raggedy-man,
Go you away, go you away
Don't you come near me today
Go and die beneath a car
Go and die beneath a tree
Raggedy-man, raggedy-man,
Don't you dare to die near me

I know, it's horrible, but that's what we used to chant every time we saw a tramp after that first time, and raggedy-man is what we always called tramps. They'd get fed up with us eventually, and would shake a fist at us, or roar in a terrifying way, but they never did us any harm. We reckoned without the power of words. When the police found a dead tramp by the roadside, crushed by a car, we all thought we were to blame. We swore we'd never chant at a raggedy-man again, but we did, of course. As we grew older, we learned that tramps were ordinary men, just like our fathers, but down on their luck for some reason.

So, after all these years I'd found myself a raggedy-man again—or he'd found me. But my day in the office, thinking about delivering parcels for on-line retailers and dealing with complaints was so busy that I didn't give him another thought until I was heading home.

Having reached the edge of the woods, I held back for at least a minute before stepping across the tree line. I'd never done that before, but then I asked myself if I really wanted to encounter that man again. I enjoy the walk home after a day sitting at my desk, and my gait is normally unhurried but reasonably sprightly, just as it had been that night, until I reached the trees. But then, as I walked among the dark trees, my feet felt like blocks of lead, they were heavy and unwilling. Telling myself to stop being illogical, after all, what was there to fear on a route I knew so well, except the old raggedy-man—and I'd already decided that he couldn't harm me. With that thought in mind, my feet returned to normal and my walk gathered pace.

I guess I'd reached the point where I'd paused the previous night, it's difficult to be exact in the darkness, when I heard the raggedy-man's voice again.

"You saw it, I know you saw it." He called, over and over. "You saw it, I know you saw it. You saw it, I know you saw it. You saw it, I know you saw it."

Again I paused, and shone my smartphone torch around me. I couldn't see the old man. Up, down, side to side and around I shone the light, and I saw nothing I knew shouldn't be there.

"You saw it, I know you saw it. You saw it, I know you saw it. You saw it, I know you saw it. You saw it, I know you saw it," the raggedy-man called out.

"Either leave me alone, or come and talk to me," I called back at him.

"You saw it, I know you saw it. You saw it, I know you saw it. You saw it, I know you saw it. You saw it, I know you saw it."

Annoyed, rather than frightened or concerned, I returned my phone to my pocket, and continued my walk home.

Within a few minutes, I could see the streetlights along the roadside, and a few minutes later I was entering my home. All the way I'd heard the raggedy-man's taunting call, diminishing with distance, until finally the soft thud of my door closing cut it off.

This routine continued day after day for about two weeks, it became as familiar as birdsong in the mornings, or the rush of car tyres along the nearby road. Then four nights ago, from when I am now, I stepped into the woods on my homeward walk, and instantly knew something was different. I felt as though the trees had closed in around me, as if with some malevolent intent. I could feel their branches reaching for me, and then their sighs of exasperation as I evaded them. I tripped more than once as my feet found exposed roots that hadn't been there before. Even the undergrowth that lived beneath the tree canopy seemed to be against me. Struggling on, I began to know fear in those woods for the very first time. Then I heard the raggedy-man calling, and, oddly, that was now so normal that I welcomed the sound of his voice and drew some comfort from it.

"You saw it, I know you saw it. You saw it, I know you saw it. You saw it, I know you saw it. You saw it, I know you saw it."

I know this is all extremely illogical, but it belongs here.

Then the raggedy-man stepped out in front me, perhaps ten feet from where I was, still repeating his pointless words.

"You want to talk?" I asked as my torch illuminated his face, his string-tied overcoat and his Doc Martens.

"You saw it, I know you saw it. You saw it, I know you saw it. You saw it, I know you saw it. You saw it, I know you saw it."

He pointed upwards, and I shone the beam in the direction indicated by his finger. Hanging there from the branch of a tree, twisting slightly, his face deformed by strangulation, but still recognisable, was the raggedy-man. I shone the beam back and forth from the hanged man, to the man before me. They were the same person, I swear it.

I can't remember what my reaction was, exactly. Panic. Fear. Horror. Dread. Probably something of all of them.

"You saw it, I know you saw it. You saw it, I know you saw it. You saw it, I know you saw it. You saw it, I know you saw it." He pointed upwards again as he spoke.

My instinctive reaction was to run, instead, I looked up again, forgetting to use my torch. There beside the hanged man was a circle of faintly glowing light. I'm convinced it's the same thing I saw briefly in the light of my torch all those weeks ago. Can I prove that? No, but I am convinced nonetheless. As I watched it began to turn, gaining speed and extruding itself towards the chanting raggedy-man. He stood and he chanted, he showed no fear.

Looking like a mini-tornado, the whatever it was touched the raggedy-man and then slipped down over him, twisting his form like a stick of sugar candy as it went. The chanting ceased, the extrusion of light withdrew, and then the circle withdrew into itself and was gone.

The woods were quiet again, the sense of dread I'd felt when I'd first stepped among the trees had left me. I slipped my phone back into my pocket, and continued walking home.

"You saw it, I know you saw it. You saw it, I know you saw it. You saw it, I know you saw it. You saw it, I know you saw it."

I heard the words again as I walked, but soft and sighing, as I imagined they might have sounded coming from the lips of the raggedy-man who'd strangled as he hung from that tree branch.

When I reached home, I called the police, and told them there was a hanged man in the woods. I told them where to look, relative to the entrance road of the housing development. Several hours later, they came to my door and said they'd found nothing. They said it was probably just a trick of the night.

******

If you've read this far, whoever you are, you might wonder why I've written all this down. Perhaps you think it's a work of fiction, although I can assure you it's not.

I don't walk through the woods by night now, I come home on the bus or cadge a ride from a colleague, but on bright sunny mornings it's still a pleasant walk. In fact, I was even beginning to think about walking home again in the evenings, but then something happened.

One morning, I awoke at about three a.m. with sounds and images from a vivid dream still in my mind. It was about the raggedy-man of course, as all my dreams seemed to be. I was lying on my back, eyes wide open, when in the ceiling corner, by the widow, a glowing disc of light appeared. It was smaller than a saucer. I swear it was the same phenomenon I'd seen in the woods. Almost of its own accord, my left arm flashed out and switched on my bedside light.

There was nothing in that corner, of course. Had it really been there, I don't know, but like the light in the woods it had vanished when confronted with a light more powerful than its own. At the moment I still think it was probably the last vestige of my dream, but I wonder... I wonder...

Reflections

When Dominic and Celina Blowfeld arrived at the small hotel they'd booked for the night, they were tempted to drive away again. Illuminated by their car headlights as they drove slowly along the narrow street, the building looked almost derelict, although, certainly, they could see lights at several upper-floor windows, and the entrance had a dim lamp glowing above its steps.

They pulled up outside the building, and looked dubiously at each other.

"Let's find somewhere else," Dominic said. He knew at once that it was an impossible suggestion, at least in this small village, and the nearest town was fifty kilometres away.

"I'm tired, you're tired, it's only for one night, let's make the best of it," Celina sensibly replied. "After all, we tried six or seven places before this one, and were told they were fully booked because of Christmas."

"You're right," Dominic said, as he switched off the car's engine and set the handbrake.

A quiet street, a tiny village, he thought, *the car will be OK here for a few hours.*

He got out of the Renault Captur, the name of which irritated him intensely, even though it was a well-built car and a pleasure to drive, crossed in front of the bonnet, and opened the passenger door to help Celina out. She was in the final stage of her first pregnancy, and had reached that point where getting into and out of a car, without assistance, was difficult. She stood beside the vehicle, pressed the palms of her hands against her lower back, and groaned. Dominic smiled at her in the dim light of the street, took her in his arms, and hugged her. He would never know what being pregnant was like, but that didn't mean that he couldn't empathise with her discomfort.

They'd left England on the previous day and crossed to France on the ferry, then headed south towards the Mediterranean coast to spend Christmas with Celina's parents. They knew they would need to break their journey somewhere, but, not knowing exactly where that would be, they hadn't booked a hotel before setting out. That had probably been a mistake, but at least they'd found this place in Saint-Georges-sur-Allier, a few kilometres off their route, and ten p.m. was late enough for the day.

He removed their suitcase from the boot of the car, and placed it by the three steps that led into the hotel, then went back and tried all the doors of the car to ensure that the central locking hadn't failed.

"I'll drop the case in reception, and then come back to help you up these steps," he said to Celina.

She smiled at him.

"Be quick," she said, "it's freezing and I think it's going to snow."

"No snow was forecast," Dominic said as he lifted the suitcase, "but you could be right. I won't be long."

At the top of the steps he pushed open the glass-paned door, and stepped inside; the door rattled shut behind him. In what passed for the reception area, a tiny space with smoke-stained walls and an old carpet on the floor, there was only a desk with an old-fashioned hotel register and a vase of withered flowers, a single dining chair, and three doors, one with the word 'Bar' inexpertly painted on a frosted glass window through which light glowed. He could hear voices and occasional laughter. After waiting for about a minute, he opened the bar door and was almost overpowered by the pall of cigarette smoke that billowed towards him. Inside the dingy room, conversation ceased and four pairs of eyes looked at him, neither hostile nor friendly, they seemed to be merely curious.

"Hotel," he said to the small, Picasso-like man behind the bar.

A rush of French came back at him, spoken far too quickly for him to understand.

"I have a room booked," he said.

"Ah, you are English," the man spoke slowly, but his English was surprisingly good. "We have no rooms, you must go elsewhere."

"Blowfeld," Dominic said, a hint of alarm in his voice, "I called you and you reserved a room. Mr and Mrs Blowfeld."

"Ah, Mr Blowfeld, why did you not say what was your name." The man came from behind the bar and ushered Dominic back into the reception area. He smelled like a blend of ashtray and beer, and was wearing ancient jeans, that sagged almost everywhere that he didn't sag himself, and a thick woollen sweater that might have been navy-blue or black in colour. "Of course I have the room for you—but where is your wife?"

"I must help her up the steps," Dominic said, as he opened the entrance door, "she is going to have a baby—very soon."

Outside, he found Celina shivering from cold. A few flakes of snow fell desultorily from the sky, and his outgoing breath hung momentarily in front of his face before vanishing.

"What took you so long?" Celina asked. Dominic thought he had been gone all of four minutes. "It's cold and creepy out here. My coat isn't warm enough for this."

"At least we have a room, and it feels nice and warm in there."

He held her steady as, one by one, she climbed up the three steps. More snow was falling now, and it was settling on the road and cold surfaces. Celina sighed with relief as she went inside, and Dominic closed the door behind her.

"Sign your name here, Mr Blowfeld, and your passport number also," the man tapped the register as he spoke. He continued to speak as Dominic fished his passport from a pocket, and signed the register. "Your room is number four, you are lucky, it is my last room. You must share the bathroom with the other rooms, it is the door between rooms two and three. For petit dejeuner—for breakfast, you must go to the café along the road. It is the only place. I wish you good sleep. The stairs are through that door, there is a switch for the light." He pointed to the door at the back of the reception area, then returned to the bar and closed the door behind him. A few moments later he opened the bar door again. "If you would like beer or wine, please to come," he said.

"We are tired," Dominic and Celina said in unison as they shook their heads, both having decided that the last thing they needed was an hour or two in a room full of cigarette smoke.

"Goodnight then," the man said, as he closed the door again.

Before they'd even moved from where they stood, they heard laughter from the bar, and guessed that they were the subjects of the man's humour.

****

Later, in their room, after they'd struggled up the narrow staircase, after they'd used the shared bathroom, they looked at each other and sighed.

"It could be worse," Celina said, "and it's only for one night."

"True," Dominic replied. "In fact, it's better than I feared. At least the bedlinen is clean, the bed feels comfortable and the smell of cigarette smoke is hardly noticeable."

"And it's thankfully warm," Celina added.

They changed into their pyjamas, as was their habit. At home they always slept naked, away from home they always dressed for bed.

Celina eased herself between the white cotton sheets, while Dominic went to the window and peered outside.

"It's still snowing he said, but I don't think it will come to much, the forecasters would have mentioned it."

"These sheets smell like sea air," Celina said, "so fresh."

"We should try to leave early in the morning," Dominic said.

"Yes. I like the sea."

"I know you do. We can get breakfast on the road, we don't have to eat in this village."

"The sound of the waves is like music, I hear them in my head and I want to sleep."

"If we leave around eight, we could be almost there by lunch time."

"It's such a restful sound."

"We need petrol too, as soon as we can."

There was no response from Celina, and Dominic realised that, as was so often the case, their thoughts had been in different places. His wife had already fallen asleep. It didn't matter. She needed to sleep for two.

He tugged the curtains back together, and walked around the bed to turn off the main room light at the switch by the door. He glimpsed himself in his pyjamas as he passed a large, black-framed mirror that hung on the wall. He thought how ludicrous he looked. He paused for a moment and stared into his own eyes, they were still very blue. He didn't think he looked like a man just touching thirty.

With the room only illuminated now by the bedside reading lamp, he passed the mirror again. It reflected what light there was, and seemed to magnify it, as though it had an inner radiance of its own, light it had held back from when the room was brighter. He knew that was impossible. He paused again, and looked again, expecting to see a dimmer version of himself looking back at him. What he saw though, while certainly a reflection of their room, was like a time-aged sepia photograph, and the face that looked at him was not his own, but that of a woman. She appeared to be about forty years old, there were small wrinkles at the corners of her eyes. She was attractive in an austere way, her lips were set firm and showed no hint of a smile, her dark hair was pulled tight to her head. He was no expert on the dress of a century ago, but her clothing, to him, suggested the nineteen-twenties. Dominic thought he saw her move, when he blinked and looked again, she was still, but a tear he was certain hadn't been there before, was mid-way down her left cheek.

He switched on the main light again, then returned to the mirror. All he saw was what he should have expected to see—the room, his own face and his pyjamas. *One more look*, he thought, as he turned the light off, *one more look*. He returned to the mirror, but nothing had changed.

Putting what he thought he'd seen in the mirror down to tiredness, he got into the bed beside his wife and draped an arm protectively across her; she moved a little, but didn't wake up. Lulled by the rhythm of Celina's breathing, he was soon asleep.

When he awoke suddenly, not to a bleary-eyed slow awareness, but a state of full wakefulness, and checked his watch, he saw that about five hours had passed. He closed his eyes again, but had difficulty rediscovering sleep, so he left the bed and quietly stood by the window. When he parted the curtains slightly, he was surprised to see that the snow that was not supposed to happen was still falling. What he could see of the village was in total darkness, not a street-light, not a house light showed anywhere.

His mind was troubled by vestiges of a dream that he had tried to push away. He could see the woman in the mirror. He heard a rough, male voice shouting. He heard the woman crying.

He went and stood in front of the mirror again. He looked and looked for what might lie beyond the glass, something that would explain what he had seen, but saw nothing that helped.

How long he stood there he didn't know, but when he heard Celina's voice he jumped.

"I think our baby wants to be born here," she said, "contractions have started and my waters have broken."

Dominic hurried to the bedside and looked at her. She'd thrown the covers aside. Around her a large, wet stain had spread across the sheet.

"Are you sure you didn't..." his words trailed off.

"No," she said, with a small laugh, "I didn't pee myself."

"Why didn't you call me sooner?"

"I wanted to be sure," she said, "this is my first time too you know."

He took her hand and squeezed it in a reassuring way, then took her face between both his hands and gave her a lingering kiss.

"We're going to be parents, we're going to be parents, we're going to be parents," he chanted, then realising that he sounded silly, he became business-like. "I'll see if I can find the owner, ask him where the doctor lives."

"Why were you standing in front of that mirror?" She asked. "Are you becoming vain?"

"Oh, no real reason. I got out of bed to stretch my legs after I woke up and couldn't get back to sleep, and I was thinking how different everything looks when it's flipped."

"Silly boy," Celina said.

****

With the aid of overhead, motion-detector lights that flickered on as he moved about, Dominic wandered the single corridor on which the hotel rooms were, then he went downstairs to check the bar. He was looking for the owner's apartment. On his way, he checked the third door in the reception area, but it was only a store-cupboard.

He found the light switch easily, to the right of the bar door as he opened it, and the room filled with the same kind of yellow light he'd seen earlier. The place reeked of stale tobacco smoke, but at least no cloud descended onto him. He spotted a door to the right of the bar counter, and as he crossed the room, he saw a small board tacked to the door, 'logement privé' it read.

"This is very bad, very bad, I was asleep," the hotelier said crossly when he finally opened the door after Dominic had banged heavily upon it at least half a dozen times. "What is it? What do you want?"

"My wife is going to have our baby, very soon. She needs a doctor."

"A doctor? At this time. The doctor is twenty kilometres away, the snow is deep, he will not come tonight."

"It's an emergency, she is in labour."

"There is nothing I can do, go and be with your wife."

"She needs someone with her, someone who knows what to expect."

"I cannot…" the man began to say, "but wait, there is a woman who might help you. I will send my wife to get her."

Dominic took the man's hand and shook it vigorously as the man tried to squirm away.

"Thank you, thank you," he said.

****

Next morning it was barely light by nine o'clock, the sky was steel grey and snow was still falling.

Celina was asleep. Their daughter was in a makeshift crib, beside her mother. She was warmly wrapped in a white shawl embroidered with blue and pink motifs, for a boy, or for a girl, one of the things they'd brought with them from England, just in case. They'd decided to call her Snow, it seemed right somehow.

Dominic sat in the room's single chair, his legs stretched out, his head tilted back. He was tired. He reflected on the events of the last few hours.

When the village woman had arrived with the hotelier's wife, and saw how advanced Celina's labour was, she did all she could to make the birth as easy as possible. She told them that she had four children of her own, and Celina told him later that she was almost as good as the midwife she'd been seeing.

"This is the first birth in our village for fifty, sixty years," the woman said as she made the sign of the cross in front of herself.

"How can that be?" Dominic asked.

"It has become our tradition that those close to their time should go to the nearest town to give birth—the facilities are there."

"Then they return to this village?"

"No, they stay away until their children are learning to walk."

Dominic thought that was odd, but he asked the woman nothing more. When they were alone, he asked Celina if she found the custom odd, but she'd replied only that birthing customs are different all over the world.

They would be in the hotel for at least a week, he thought, and would miss Christmas with Celina's parents at their retirement home near Nice. They were both disappointed by that, particularly Dominic, as Celina's father was gradually educating him in the finer points of wine appreciation. Once Celina could travel, they had decided to return to England for the baby's sake.

Celina would sleep a lot, but he didn't know what he would do to kill time in the hotel day after day—at least it had a bar.

A knock on the door shattered his reverie, and Dominic got up from his chair to see who it was.

"I am Father Pierre," the rotund man at the door said. "I have been sent to bless your child."

"Sent? By whom?"

"By the woman who helped your wife."

Without waiting, the priest pushed his way into the room. He paused briefly by the mirror, glanced sideways at it, and then crossed himself.

"As I feared," he muttered, "this birth is a very bad thing, very bad."

"What do you mean?" Dominic asked.

"It's our tradition to discourage those with child from giving birth here," the priest echoed the village woman's words, then crossed to the crib, opened his Bible, and read something in French too fast for Dominic to follow. "In nomine Patris et fillii et Spiritus Sancti," he concluded.

"What did you say?"

"Just a blessing in God's name," Father Pierre replied, "and I hope it protects your daughter. Goodbye." He crossed himself again as he passed the mirror, and then left the room.

Another village tradition, Dominic thought, then he recalled that there were never any new-born infants in the village.

****

That night, Dominic persuaded the hotelier to give him a folding bed on which to sleep, so as not to disturb Celina. The day had passed slowly—in fact it had dragged. Eventually he'd succumbed to the charms of the smoky bar, where he'd had several beers and tried to converse using his imperfect French.

He'd left when his lungs could stand no more cigarette smoke, and returned to the room, where mother and baby were both sleeping.

He stood for a few minutes and looked at his family, feeling both love and pride in equal measure. He now had two beautiful girls in his life. He peered briefly through the window. As far as he could tell the snow had stopped, twenty four hours after it had started.

After showering and putting on his pyjamas, he turned off the main light and was going to turn off the bedside light, when he felt drawn towards the mirror again. He stood before it and looked, the austere woman was there again, but she was different. Her lips held a hint of a smile, her eyes looked more alive. Dominic shrugged and went to turn off the bedside light, before fumbling his way to the folding bed. His sleep was fitful, he tossed and turned, experienced periods of total wakefulness, but he must have eventually slept more deeply, because it was an effort to come fully awake when he heard Celina's shrill scream bite into the still, dark morning.

He went to her as quickly as he could, as screaming still, she pointed to the empty crib beside the bed. Snow was gone, her shawl was gone, all that remained of her was the slight impression her tiny body had left.

Dominic held Celina close to him, and held her until her scream had subsided into terrible sobs. Then he cried with her.

Later, he realised that his first action, even before comforting his wife, should have been to ask the hotelier to call the police. He should have looked for signs of an intruder. There were so many possible responses, but his had been to comfort his wife.

****

They stayed in that room for one more night before the police took them to a better hotel in the nearest town. They were told not to return to England until investigations were completed. For a few days they were suspected of killing their daughter, it was no unknown for a new mother to reject a child, they were told. But a body was never found, and the virgin snow around the hotel showed that no one had left the building in the night.

About two weeks later, they were told they could return to England, that investigations would continue, but the mysterious disappearance might never be solved.

Dominic wanted to return to Saint-Georges-sur-Allier, to say goodbye to Snow in the room from which she had vanished. Celina cried and didn't want to go, so he went alone.

In the street outside the hotel, Father Pierre hurried up to him.

"I am so sorry," the priest said, "I am so sorry that God's blessing did not save your daughter."

"Save her? What do you mean, father?"

"Saint-Georges-sur-Allier lost many new born before nineteen-sixty, that is why our tradition became that children should not be born here. Forty, fifty, sixty babies vanished, no one knows for sure. The Police were never able to find them."

"And you think that after a break of fifty years or more my daughter has become one of this number?" Dominic almost laughed.

"That is what I think. I believe there is something evil about this place that takes babes from their mothers. Some of the older villagers think it is the ghost of a woman who used to live in the house that is now our hotel. It is said that she never bore him a living son or daughter, and in a fit of rage he murdered her. She is said to have suffered nine miscarriages or stillborn. What caused god to visit such a punishment upon her no one knows."

"A scary story for winter nights," Dominic said.

"It is more than that, I fear," Father Pierre said over his shoulder, as he sloshed away in thawing snow.

Dominic went to the hotel, and asked if he could see room four. The hotelier reluctantly agreed, and handed him the key.

"I think you must pay me for the mattress also, it was ruined you know."

It was Dominic's turn to be reluctant, but he pulled two-hundred Euros from his wallet and handed them to the man, before going up to the room.

He felt odd being back in room four. He didn't feel anything he could recognise as his daughter, but then they had hardly known her. In fact, he was disappointed to acknowledge, he felt nothing at all other than a small twinge of sadness.

He sat on the edge of the bed and looked around. Nothing had changed, probably not even the mattress, but he couldn't be bothered to check. He caught his reflection in the mirror, and stood in front of it. He could see a grey hair or two; at thirty that seemed far too soon. He crossed to the window and pulled the curtains across to darken the room a little. Then he returned to the mirror and looked at himself looking back at him. He wondered why he had done that. He wondered what Celina would say if she could see him now.

As he watched, his reflection in the mirror began to fade, as if something behind it was pushing through. Little by little the austere woman appeared, but she no longer looked austere. Her hair was attractively styled, her clothes were colourful, there was a twinkle in her eyes, and a real smile on her lips. The drab sepia-tones had gone, replaced by the colours of a living world. In her arms she held a small child. The tiny form was wrapped in a white shawl, embroidered with motifs in blue and pink, for a boy, or for a girl.

Dominic wanted to scream, but no sound would come. His eyes lost focus for a moment, and when they refocussed he saw a single tear on the smiling woman's left cheek. It flowed slowly down, and when he tasted salt in the corner of his mouth he realised that the tear was a reflection of his own.

Petals

Later, when he'd raked the petals of the flowering cherry trees into neat little piles that would have pleased Elizabeth, he stopped for a moment to think about where his day had gone.

He remembered reading his newspaper over morning coffee; it was delivered every day, and when he heard it drop through the letter-box and onto the doormat he knew it was time to get out of bed. Elizabeth had always called him when his coffee and toast were ready, and when the jar of Frank Cooper's thick cut marmalade was precisely placed for him. But since Elizabeth had died, he'd had to take care of those details himself.

He recalled the newspaper's headline that morning, something gloomy about war in a far off country, and as he'd read the report that followed, his rheumy eyes had filled with tears at the thought of dead babies and starving children. He'd put his newspaper aside, and had immediately called Oxfam to make a sizeable donation, money that he'd hoped would make life easier for some, for a few days at least. He did this quite often; after all, he had more money than he would ever need.

When his daughter, Eloise, found out, she would berate him and tell him that he was a silly old man, and that he was frittering away her inheritance on people who didn't deserve his help. Because of this, they seldom saw each other nowadays, he had trouble remembering how old his grandchildren were, and loneliness had long been lodged in his heart. Occasionally, he would telephone Eloise, just to remind himself that he still had a family, but those calls would always end with her harsh words and her voice abruptly disappearing.

After breakfast, he'd taken a walk in the nearby woods. He couldn't remember whether he'd seen anyone else or not, or exchanged a polite good morning with a stranger, but he remembered hearing the bark of a dog. When he returned home, it wasn't yet lunchtime, so he'd made a cup of instant coffee and carried it through to the south facing conservatory, where he sat in a pool of warm, spring sunlight.

After that, time ceased to exist for him until he looked at his wristwatch and saw that it was almost four in the afternoon—and that his coffee was cold.

"I miss you, dear, I really miss you," he'd said aloud when he saw a shadow move, but it was only a bird on a shrub. He smiled ruefully at his silliness, and thought that perhaps Eloise was right, that he was just a silly old man. Then he went out into the garden, took up the lawn rake that was resting against one of the flowering cherry trees, and raked the fallen petals into the neat little piles that were before him now.

When Elizabeth was alive, this had been a seasonal ritual, and although he now thought the sprinkle of pink and white petals across the lawn looked attractive, he maintained the ritual because he felt, he believed, that doing so kept him close to his wife. He knew she would approve, and if she were present now, she would be expecting him to gather the petals into a refuse bag and then empty them out onto the compost heap that was hidden behind a hedge at the end of the garden. So that's exactly what he did.

On his way to the compost heap he came to the shaded corner of the garden where Eloise's childhood pets had always been buried when they died. He remembered that Eloise had insisted that they conduct proper funeral ceremonies, with a prayer and a hymn and the shedding of tears. He thought that five, or was it six, of his daughter's pets had been buried here over a period of fifteen years or so, each small grave, with its own wooden marker, now vanished among the weeds that he had never been able to remove. There was Miaow, the cat, Squeak, the guinea pig, Burble, the goldfish, Tweet, the budgerigar, Thumper, the rabbit—and there was the very first one, a small dog that had been run over by a mail van in the lane the passed by the house, that was—but he couldn't remember the dog's name, and it bothered him—it bothered him even more than not knowing where his day had gone.

****

"What do you want, daddy?" Eloise's voice was hectoring in tone, even before he'd said a word, but that was her way.

"I just want to hear your voice," he replied, "we haven't spoken for a while you know." He knew there was no chance that his daughter would feel guilty.

"I haven't got time to talk now, daddy."

"When will you have time? Time is all I have, and I'm so lonely since your mother died."

"I don't know when I'll have time. You should go into one of those homes for old people like you. You'll have plenty of company there. I must go."

"Just one thing, dear," he said quickly, "what was your little dog's name, the one we buried in the garden. I can't remember."

"You're becoming senile, daddy. He was called Barker, you know that," Eloise said crossly.

Then her voice was gone, the line was dead, just as it always was. She had spared him less than two minutes of her time.

But yes, he thought, *Barker, I remember Barker, he was a sweet little dog.*

****

That evening, he looked at the ready-meals stacked in his freezer, but couldn't be bothered to heat one for his dinner, even though he'd eaten nothing other than two slices of toast all day. Instead, he dissolved a vegetable Oxo cube in a mug of hot water and thought of it as soup.

As he sat at the kitchen table, waiting for his drink to cool, he thought about Elizabeth and about Eloise. He couldn't understand how mother and daughter could be so different. They looked like twins born thirty-five years apart, but while Elizabeth was kindness and caring, Eloise was selfishness and uncaring. He doubted that his daughter cared for anyone but herself, and perhaps her two sons.

"Where did we go wrong?" He asked aloud. "Where did we go wrong?"

He sipped his Oxo, and found it thin but tasty.

"I miss you, dear, I really miss you," he'd said aloud again, when he saw a shadow move, just as he had earlier. Then he realised that the only shadow in the kitchen that could move was his own, and again he thought that perhaps Eloise was right, that he was just a silly old man.

He felt a warmth against his face, he smelled the scent of flowering cherry trees.

"You're not a silly old man," a voice said, "you care too much."

"Elizabeth, is that you?"

"It's who you most want it to be," the voice said.

"I want it to be you, Elizabeth, only you."

He wasn't sure whether he was speaking aloud, hearing a real voice, or imagining these things like a silly old man. He looked at his Oxo, steam had stopped rising from the cup. The fragrance of flowering cherry trees grew stronger, the warmth against his cheek more familiar.

"You did well with the petals today, you did so well."

"I did it for you, Elizabeth, for you."

"I know, I know."

His eyes began to lose focus, he could see nothing clearly. He looked at his watch, to see what time it was. *I have nothing but time*, he thought.

"I think it's time you came to be with me," the words were gentle, they caressed his mind, took away his loneliness. "Would you like that?"

"Yes," he said, "yes, I'd like that so much."

Then he leaned forward and rested his head on his arm. He thought he should finish his Oxo, but instead he closed his eyes and knew that he would never feel lonely again.

Scratching

Bradley awoke at three in the morning to the sound of insistent scratching against the glass door that led onto the tiny balcony of his bedroom.

He'd heard the noise before and it reminded him of the childhood sound of his pet cat scratching to be let in—the soft thump as a paw hit the glass and then the squeaking sound as claws were raked down the window's surface. Every few nights the sound occurred. Usually he ignored it and went back to sleep, but tonight, as he listened, it began to irritate him.

Doing his best not to disturb Mara, who breathed shallowly, regularly, deep asleep beside him, he eased himself from the bed and crossed to the door. Only the glow of their alarm clock and street light creeping in around the blind illuminated the room.

As he pulled the edge of the blind towards him, something moved at the edge of his vision. He turned his head slightly, but there was nothing on the balcony to focus on except the dim presence of the low wall and wrought ironwork that enclosed it on three sides, whatever he had seen was gone. He pressed his forehead against the cold glass and peered into a night that was filled with darkness, the looming shapes of nearby buildings, glimmering street lights and the rain that had been falling incessantly since early afternoon. It struck him as odd that there were no moving headlights passing along the street—there was always traffic in the city—but he dismissed the thought and returned to his bed.

Struggling to find sleep again he wondered what had caused the sound that had awakened him. He could dismiss the movement as his own dark reflection against the night, but the scratching sound was real, it was real, it wasn't his imagination. What was more, he was convinced that each time he heard it, it was a little louder. With this thought wriggling in his mind, time passed slowly; it was three thirty, two hours later it was four fifteen, then it was four twenty-five. He turned the clock so that he could no longer see its glowing hands and numerals and eventually fell asleep again..

****

"I heard it again," Bradley said to Mara over breakfast.

He was eating sweet cereal, she was peeling and slicing an apple, mugs of freshly made coffee steamed before them.

"Heard what, Brad?"

"Bradley!" He enunciated loudly. She knew how much use of the short form of his name annoyed him, it made him sound like something a carpenter used.

"Oh, the scratching noise."

"Yes, the scratching noise!"

It was a bad start. He knew that being irritable early on meant he would be irritable all day.

"I think you're imagining it Brad..."

"Bradley, for God's sake, Bradley!"

"... whenever I spend the night here I never hear anything."

"That's because you sleep like a log, I'm a shallow sleeper. Next time I hear it and you're here I'll wake you up."

"Don't bother Brad, you know how bad tempered I get when my sleep is disturbed.

"Bradley! Bradley! Bradley! Fucking Bradley. Don't you get it?"

"Get what, Brad?" She smiled.

He slammed down his coffee mug, glared at Mara and angrily headed for the bathroom. Mara, as usual, had left toothpaste and hair in the basin and he felt his anger increasing. They'd only known each other for a few month and already he knew their relationship was doomed.

When he'd finished in the bathroom he returned to the kitchen, but Mara had already left. No goodbye. No affectionate note. She'd just left.

****

It was two nights later that he heard the scratching sound again.

He listened for a minute or two as its insistence grew, then closed his eyes on the darkened room and went back to sleep. This was the pattern of his nocturnal awakenings for the next three weeks.

He spoke to Mara a number of times, he called her, she called him. He was gentle with her even when she called him 'Brad'. He agreed that they would see each other again, but neither of them made an effort to arrange anything. When the calls ceased altogether Bradley realised that Mara was like his other girlfriends of recent years, a fling that was mostly enjoyable while it lasted, but that quickly ended and was never revisited.

One night in the fourth week he woke to a sound at three o'clock, the usual hour—whatever it was, was very precise at least—but it was more than the usual scratching. The sound of claws on glass was there, but it was accompanied by an insistent tapping that seemed urgent. To Bradley it sounded as if something had come loose and was being buffeted against his door by a night-time breeze, even though it was a clear, still night.

He left from his bed and crossed to the balcony door to investigate for the first time in almost a month. He wanted the sound to stop. The scratching was familiar, he could live with it, but the tap-tap-tap-tap, tap-tap-tap-tap, was so even, so metronomic that he knew he wouldn't be able to sleep through it.

Lifting the edge of the blind he saw a flash of movement, dark on dark, and the noises ceased.

He slid the glass door aside and stepped out onto the balcony. Chilly night air embraced him and sent a momentary shiver through him. Small, potted conifers, barely reflected in the dark glass, stood like sentries each side of the door. Other than these there was nothing on the balcony. He thought that maybe he could put a chair out here in the summer, but at little more than one metre by three the balconies were not good for much and struck him as a rather pointless adornment on this utilitarian 1960s apartment block. There were no grand vistas here, no mountains or forests, no heaving seas to watch—in fact the only view was of other carbuncular buildings thrown up with no consideration of the city's aesthetics.

Bradley looked at the sky, it was a starry autumn night with no visible moon. It was quiet. On nearby buildings lights twinkled, but there were few of them. Crossing to the rail he looked down on the traffic free street, then he went back inside, fastened the sliding door and returned to his cold bed.

Over the following nights the scratching and tapping sounds occurred more often, always at the same time, always ceasing if he could be bothered to investigate, never lasting more than thirty minutes if he stayed in bed. So much a part of his nightly routine had the sounds become that on the nights when the sounds did not occur Bradley awoke at three o'clock anyway, and wondered if they had come early.

****

"Yes, other tenants in that apartment have sometimes reported strange noises in the night... not everyone mind you." the building manager told Bradley one morning.

"Like the noises I hear, scratching and tapping on the balcony door?"

"Oh no, those noises are new. I know of chattering voices, a loudly purring cat, heavy sighs—and not always from the balcony. Someone once reported that their bed was rocking like a boat on water, and someone else that choking smoke had appeared in the bedroom—from nowhere."

"Why wasn't I told of these things?" Bradley asked.

"I tried to tell you, but all you were interested in securing the place before the low rent attracted others. That's why the rent's low. People never stay long. You've been here almost three months now, that makes you a stayer."

Bradley thought about what the manager had just told him, he thought also about the low rent that had attracted him to the apartment, and decided he could tolerate the noises.

"I guess I'll stay for now," he said.

"Me, I put it all down to over-active imaginations, watching too many horror movies. The whole place has been checked out you know, there's nothing there. Even the police gave it a good going over after..." the manager's words trailed off.

"After what?"

"It doesn't matter," the manager said, "it's nothing." Then he looked away from Bradley and attended to make-believe work.

****

He'd thought about the building manager's unfinished sentence on and off throughout the day as he shuffled papers and dealt with 'phone calls. Cut short, as the man's words were, it was as if he'd realised that he was about to say something that might upset his 'stayer'.

After three months in the apartment Bradley was on nodding terms with several other residents on his floor, a nod and an occasional 'good morning' or 'terrible weather isn't it' or 'good evening'—never a real conversation—was all they exchanged. As he was, the people who lived Wormwood House were private, unpushy, quiet—above all quiet—who locked themselves and their secrets behind their institutionally off-white doors whenever they were at home.

He decided that the next time he saw one of his neighbours he would be outgoing—friendly even—and engage them in a proper conversation to try and find out if they knew anything about his apartment. That's if any of them were prepared to talk.

Arriving home that evening he noticed the building manager, who always seemed to be on duty, scuttle away from behind his desk and into the room where he kept all the mysterious things he needed in his work. Bradley knew the man was hiding from him, and he called out a cheery, taunting, I know where you are greeting as he walked across the lobby to collect his mail on the way to the elevator.

On the seventh floor he walked the corridor towards his own door, pausing momentarily, listening, at each door he passed. He heard only the almost inaudible click as the motion detecting ceiling lights glimmered on as he approached and faded off as he passed, casting a series of monochrome shadows before him like frames from a slowly turning movie reel.

Safely inside his apartment, with the door safely locked and his secrets safe for another night, he crossed to the window of his living room and peered out over the stardust lights of the city. It looked like a cold night, but even though he had been outside five minutes ago he couldn't remember whether it was cold or not. He pulled the window blind down to shut out the night and then went into his bedroom and did the same.

In the four hours between arriving home and his habitual eleven o'clock bedtime he heated and ate a supermarket ready-meal, looked at the mail he'd collected in the lobby, watched a documentary on TV and read a few pages of a book. As he cleaned his teeth he couldn't remember what he'd eaten, who his mail was from, what the documentary was about or what he'd read. It pained him to realise that the routines of his life had become so much a part of him that he didn't even remember the detail of them. He had never thought his life would be like this. As always, he had hoped for a call from Mara, but no call came.

****

Tap-tap-tap-tap, tap-tap-tap-tap, tap-tap-tap-tap!
Scritt-scritt-thump, Scritt-scritt-thump, Scritt-scritt-thump!
Bradley didn't need to check the time. He pulled his quilt over his head and tried to ignore the noises.
Tap-tap-tap-tap, tap-tap-tap-tap, tap-tap-tap-tap!
Scritt-scritt-thump, Scritt-scritt-thump, Scritt-scritt-thump!
Tap-tap-tap-tap, tap-tap-tap-tap, tap-tap-tap-tap!
Scritt-scritt-thump, Scritt-scritt-thump, Scritt-scritt-thump!
He sighed as he threw back the bedclothes and padded across the carpeted floor to the balcony door.

He lifted the edge of the blind just as he always did.

He saw buildings silhouetted, dark on dark, just as he always did. He noticed the trafficless street, just as he always did.

He knew something had darted away from the periphery of his vision—just as it always did.

This no longer frightened him. It was just another routine, albeit a strange one, that was becoming more and more a part of his life.

****

Three more months passed.

In that time Bradley became so accustomed to the night-time noises that on several occasions he didn't wake up at all, although he was sure his visitor had called... just as it always did. On most nights though, so expectant was he, that he awoke in anticipation of the noises at a few minutes before three o'clock.

Tonight was one of those nights. He checked the time—it was four minutes before three—and propped himself up on an elbow as he mentally counted off the seconds. He was off by five seconds.

Tap-tap-tap-tap, tap-tap-tap-tap, tap-tap-tap-tap!

Scritt-scritt-thump, Scritt-scritt-thump, Scritt-scritt-thump!

Tap-tap-tap-tap, tap-tap-tap-tap, tap-tap-tap-tap!

Scritt-scritt-thump, Scritt-scritt-thump, Scritt-scritt-thump!

He heard the familiar sounds and was determined that tonight he would not leave his bed to look.

Tap-tap-tap-tap, tap-tap-tap-tap, tap-tap-tap-tap!

Scritt-scritt-thump, Scritt-scritt-thump, Scritt-scritt-thump!

Tap-tap-tap-tap, tap-tap-tap-tap, tap-tap-tap-tap!

Scritt-scritt-thump, Scritt-scritt-thump, Scritt-scritt-thump!

His resolve began to waver, but he stayed in his bed.

Tap-brad-tap-ley-tap-tap, tap-brad-tap-ley-tap-tap, tap-brad-tap-ley-tap-tap!

Scritt-scritt-thump, Scritt-scritt-thump, Scritt-scritt-thump!

Tap-brad-tap-ley-tap-tap, tap-brad-tap-ley-tap-tap, tap-brad-tap-ley-tap-tap!

Scritt-scritt-thump, Scritt-scritt-thump, Scritt-scritt-thump!

As Bradley heard the whisper of his name subsumed in the tapping and scratching against his window, he rushed from his bed, crossed the room and pulled the blind fully up.

His eyes took a few seconds to adjust to the darkness. Nothing moved away from the periphery of his vision. Nothing was not quite seen, the noises stopped. A light rain was falling, there was no traffic on the street below.

A faintly luminescent spot floated towards him. By the time it was over his balcony it was an orb the size of a human head. In his mind he saw Mara's face.

"Mara, Mara," he said as he slid the balcony door aside, "Mara."

It was cold outside and his thin cotton pyjamas were no protection against the rain.

"Mara, Mara, Mara."

He was standing directly in front of the floating orb.

He stared. He saw small sparks of electricity flashing across the orb.

"You're not Mara," his voice was little more than a whisper, but to him it sounded as if he had shouted.

He tried to turn and go back into his bedroom, but it felt as if a giant hand was squeezing him tightly.

He began to rise above the tiled surface of the balcony. He slowly followed the orb as it backed away. He passed over the wrought iron railings and knew that only the street was beneath him.

Suddenly the orb sped away and the pressure that held him was released.

Bradley was falling. Falling. Falling.

He started to scream, then stopped.

Four seconds is a long time, he knew that was an irrational thought.

In the darkness he could barely see the rush of buildings rising as he fell. He felt the cold. He felt the rain.

He was glad it was night, he was glad there were no people on the street below at least he would hurt no-one as...

****

"Morning Mrs Oliver," the building manager said when a woman passed him on the steps as she left Wormwood House.

The police had cordoned off the front of the building. They stood and scratched their chins.

"Another one!" Mrs Oliver said. "So sad... that makes..."

"Four" That makes four Mrs Oliver."

Mrs Oliver moved on, to go about her business whatever it was.

Staring at the huge bloodstain where Bradley's body had landed the building manager smiled, He knew it wouldn't be there long.

"The council will soon wash that away," he said to no one, "then I can let that apartment again."

Half-Turns

My father would never buy me a wristwatch when I was a kid. He said I would become too obsessed with the passing of time.

Our lives were instead regulated by the single clock in our house, and I would watch my father wind it at seven o'clock every evening, as soon as it had finished it's chiming. To him, the winding was like a religious ritual. He would lift the clock from its shelf—a kitchen shelf so high up that I couldn't see anything that might be on it—flick specks of dust from its wooden case with his handkerchief, then open the glass front and insert the key. He counted aloud the number of half-turns he gave the key.

"One, two, three, four, five…"

When he reached twenty-four the winding was done. He removed the key, closed the clock front, buffed the glass with his shirt sleeve and put the clock back where I couldn't see it.

"Never over-wind a clock," he'd say, "one half-turn of the key for each hour of the day is all that's necessary. If you do that, a clock will last a lifetime and always give you the right hour of day. Isn't that so mother?"

Mother didn't answer of course, she couldn't since she had died, but father still addressed her several times each day. He said that by speaking to her she would know she was still welcome.

Although father was not one to show his emotions, as I grew older I learned that he missed mother a great deal. With me, he was always strict but loving, he cared for me well and saw that I was fed; he encouraged me with my schoolwork, even when it was obvious that in certain subjects I had reached a level that he just didn't understand. He didn't laugh, or even smile, very much. He didn't listen to the radio or read books. He refused to have a television in the house.

When I came downstairs from my bedroom of an evening, after finishing my homework, I would usually find father sitting on the sofa in the darkened parlour. As I pushed the door open he was so silent that he might have been asleep.

"What are you doing, father?" I would ask.

"What a question boy," he would reply, "I was thinking, of course, just thinking. What else would a lonely man do in a darkened room?"

"Is thinking like imagining?"

"I guess it is, in a way."

"What were you imagining, father?"

This exchange, perhaps with variations to the words we spoke, had become as much a nightly ritual as winding the clock. At this point father always sighed deeply.

"I was imagining how much better our lives would be if mother was still with us."

Then I would sit on the sofa beside him. Sometimes, when I was small, he would take my hand and hold it in his. I could feel the callouses and scars left by the constant use of tools in his work as a carpenter. His skin was rough and I came to know that they were the hands of a simple, hard-working man.

After a few minutes, father would tell me it was bed-time. A little later he would come to my room, kiss my cheek and tell me I was his good boy.

****

As I grew older, the hand holding ceased. Father didn't say why, but perhaps he felt that he should not be holding the hand of a boy on his way to becoming a man. The night-time kiss stopped too, and I was no longer told that I was his good boy. Apart from that, our lives were unchanged and our rituals were still observed with the same essential regularity as they had always been undertaken.

Eventually, of course, I went away to college, but by then I'd learned just how lonely father really was; without my company he would be lonelier still. So it was that I determined to eschew the usual student lifestyle and travel home as often as was possible. That turned out to be most weekends in fact. A sense of duty is a powerful motivating force, but returning home so often, when I should have been learning about self-reliance, wasn't only about duty because I harboured great love for my father.

My parents had decided to have a child at a time others referred to as 'late in life', my mother was past forty and father had turned fifty when I was born. I have memories of them calling me 'their little miracle', and it wasn't until I learned about human reproduction that I understood what that meant. Advances in the biological sciences have since made families 'late in life' much more common. My home was filled with sunshine and laughter all through my infant years, and it wasn't until I was about seven years old that mother became ill. Her decline was very rapid and, although she still smiled for me often, I felt the joy leave my home a little more each day. I was still cared for, I was still loved, but my parents no longer laughed.

"Your mother has gone to heaven," father said to me quite simply one day when I was eight. He didn't explain, but even at that age I could tell from the tears in his eyes that it was a sad day. All the curtains in our house were closed, and never again were they fully opened to allow the sunshine in. Some years later, I thought there must have been a funeral that I was not allowed to attend.

That's when father's loneliness began, and that's why each Friday I would leave the campus soon after lunch, if I could, and take the train to my hometown. It was a two-hour journey, with, at its end, a fifteen-minute walk to our house. As I walked the town streets, as I walked past the closed-down shops and overflowing litter-bins, none of the sour faced people I passed recognised me—or I them—and I remembered what a miserable agglomeration of humanity this had always been.

Eventually I would come to the street where we lived, it was just as miserable as the town itself, with its shabby post-war houses, the vandalised red telephone box and pot-holed road. Farther along the street, three or four children were kicking a ball about, but I didn't need to go that far.

I had difficulty pushing open the front-garden gate, partly because it was hanging off its hinges, mostly because thick tussocks of grass were growing from the path. But finally, it moved, and I walked towards windows staring at me like barely opened eyes and the familiar front door for which I had a key.

"Father," I called out as I entered the house, "it's me!"

Father's response, not much more than a grunt, came from the parlour as it always did. I left my bag at the foot of the stairs, then went and sat on the sofa next to him.

"What are you doing, father?" I asked.

"What a question boy," he replied, "I was thinking, of course, just thinking. What else would a lonely man do in a darkened room?" It was what he always said, although the room wasn't really dark at this time of day, at this time of year.

He looked much older than I remembered him being, but that was the case with every week that passed. He was over seventy now, he looked frail, his skin had a waxy sheen and his grey hair needed combing.

I stayed with him for a while, but there was no conversation, he still had no interest in newspapers or books, he still refused to have a television set.

"I'm going upstairs to study," I said after thirty minutes or so.

"As you wish," he replied.

That was at about five o'clock.

****

I was immersed in reading a book on the geography of Kalimantan when I heard the voice; it was seven o'clock and father would be preparing to wind the clock.

"Father needs you," the female voice said. "Quickly, father needs you."

Reasoning that my imagination was playing tricks on me, I returned to my reading.

"Quickly, father needs you," the voice said again. It was then that I realised it was mother's voice. As impossible at it was, it was mother's voice.

I descended the stairs two at a time and went to the kitchen. There I found father lying unconscious on the floor with his keys beside him. I knelt beside him and felt for his pulse; it was feeble through his brittle skin, and irregular.

"Wind the clock, wind the clock," mother's voice said, "quickly." Quickly had always been one of mother's favourite words.

"I need to call the doctor."

"The clock first, father will be alright, the clock first, there's a good boy."

Reluctantly, I picked up father's keys, stood up and reached for the clock. It was seven-ten, that meant father had been late for his daily ritual. He was never late winding the clock. Never. I opened the glass front and inserted the key, then began to turn. I remembered to count, exactly twenty-four half-turns were all that were necessary for good timekeeping.

"One, two, three, four, five…"

Mother's voice counted along with me. With each half-turn, father moved a little or groaned. When we reached twenty-four the winding was done, and father was sitting up watching me. I removed the key, closed the clock front, buffed the glass with my shirt sleeve—just as he father did—and put the clock back on its shelf.

"Never over-wind a clock, one half-turn of the key for each hour of the day is all that's necessary. If you do that, a clock will last a lifetime and always give you the right hour of day. That's what you always say isn't it father?" Mother's voice said.

"Is that you, mother?" Father asked. "Is it really you? I've been so lonely these past years without you, so lonely."

"It's me dear," Mother said. "I'm always here, always with you."

"I'll call the doctor," I said.

"Don't," father said, I was late winding the clock is all, and that should never be."

Mother was silent again, but we both knew she was with us still.

The Knowledge

"Do you ever think about old Jonny Swiggert?" Bobby asked me. We were standing under the awning of Sam's All-Night Coffee & Donuts, sipping hot coffee from polystyrene cups. Light rain was falling and the autumn air had a winter chill to it. A few metres away, over the parapet, the river threw up a misty haze that glistened in the almost-darkness.

"Sure I think about Jonny," I answered, "Who doesn't think about Jonny?"

"I think about Jonny too," Sam said with a yawn. "He used to stop by here several times every night, liked his coffee without sugar, strong and black... not like you two sweet toothed bastards." He laughed as he pulled a cloth from his shoulder and flicked at something imagined on the counter, then returned to rearranging things we couldn't see.

"I wonder what happened to him." Bobby's voice was thoughtful.

In reality 'old Jonny Swiggert wasn't old. He was about the same age as me... and Bobby, in his forties. We'd all joined the cab company in the same month. That was a good few years ago now. We'd done our training. We had our licenses. We could drive our fares around the city and find our way to any street.

"I reckon he just decided to start over," Sam said, "people do that you know. Like that politician a few years ago. He left his clothes on the beach and vanished."

"Jonny had a wife and kids, and a nice house. Why would he leave all that?" Bobby sipped his coffee. "He had a better life than me, and I wouldn't leave what I've got."

I listened to the two of them as they bantered back and forth. It was like this every night, Bobby and Sam got a kick out of antagonising each other, one taking an opposing stance on any issue the other raised—irrespective of what they really thought.

I finished my coffee, slapped a handful of coins onto Sam's counter, and left them to it.

"Keep the change, Sam," I called as I headed back to my cab. "See you later."

I sat and listened to dispatch for a moment or two, it was a quiet night, then I called in and said I was going to park up in a side street for a while, it was better than wasting diesel by endlessly trawling the streets for drunks and clubbers who just might want a ride, but probably didn't.

Talk of Jonny Swiggert made me think more about his disappearance. Neither he, nor his cab, had been seen in almost three years. He'd been a likable bloke, always smiling, always wanting to pass on news about his kids. A real family man he was. Why would he up and disappear like that? On that point, at least, Bobby was right, Jonny had a good life.

Parked beneath a street light my mind wandered, although I can't recall now exactly where it wandered to. Maybe I was thinking of a holiday, a hot Spanish beach, tapas, Sangria and señoritas. Maybe I was thinking of Christmas. More likely though, I was thinking of sleep. I was startled to awareness by a drunk noisily singing his way along the street. He got to my cab, unzipped his pants, and pissed against the wheels. Then he banged on the roof, pressed his face against the window, just a few inches from my face, giggled, said sorry and went on his way again, still singing merrily. Was I disgusted? Was I angry? Of course I was! But if past experience had taught me anything, it was that remonstrating with people in that state achieved nothing, so I quietly seethed for a while and decided it was time to revisit Sam's All-Night Coffee & Donuts. It was 3 a.m.

I parked beside the only other cab there. It wasn't Bobby, but old Frank. He really was old, sixty if he was a day, and he was a kind of father figure to all the younger drivers.

"Get your coffee and come talk with me, Mike," he said

through his open window as I passed, "there ain't anything else doing. I get lonely on these quiet nights."

Two minutes later I squirmed into the seat beside Frank with a steaming cup of hot, sweet coffee in my hand.

"You thinking of retiring yet, Frank?" I asked.

"What? Me? Retire? You've gotta be joking. What would I do but spend more time indoors with her what complains all the time, about everything?"

"You could take a long holiday... find a hobby."

"A holiday? This country's good enough for me lad, always has been, always will be. As for a hobby, this is my hobby as well as my work. If I did anything else I'd grow old and die."

I'd met men like Frank before. They thought work was the be all and end all of human existence. They had too little imagination to see farther than that, too little imagination to dream or yearn for something better.

"I was talking to Bobby about Jonny earlier."

"Jonny?"

"You remember Jonny, him what vanished about three years ago, cab and all."

Frank was quiet for a few moments and I imagined his face screwing up in the darkness as he tried to remember.

"Yes, I remembers Jonny now that you mention him." He let out a long sigh and then breathed in noisily.

"Strange how he just disappeared like that, never to be seen again."

"He weren't the first you know. Happened to a few blokes going back a bit. Mostly they was cabbies, but once or twice other drivers. Six or seven since I've been driving, but some of the old timers when I started used to tell of disappearances too."

"I've never heard that before."

"It's true... as true as God's a white man... as true as me sitting here, by Jesus it is."

"Why doesn't anyone investigate... the police, the company? Someone."

"Because they gave up investigating, it got them nowhere. Now all those what could investigate just prefer to hush things up."

"You mean they know where these people vanish to?"

"No, they don't know, that's the trouble. What ain't known about causes people to worry, so better to keep it quiet. So quiet that now they don't even tell the youngsters like you about it.

When I got the knowledge there was two parts to the learning. One was to learn the streets of the city that are on the maps. The other was to learn about those that ain't on any map, those narrow streets and dark alleyways that come alive at night, where no driver, no one in fact, should ever go. You've seen them, we all see them. Us older drivers knows about them and know to avoid them, but youngsters like you blank them out because they ain't part of the knowledge you learned."

"That's silly," I blurted out without thinking, "it's not possible."

"What you think don't affect what is, sonny boy. What is just is. There's a hidden city inside the city, that goes back centuries, and there's something there that no one wants to know."

"You're making all this up," I said.

"Tell you what, next time you're at the depot ask the boss—I mean the big boss, not the dispatcher or some other jumped up little twerp with power—about the old knowledge and see what happens. I've gotta go now."

I got out of Frank's cab still clutching my cooled coffee. I sipped the coffee, but it was awful. I walked across to Sam, who was rearranging things I couldn't see, flicking imagined things from his counter with a cloth pulled off his shoulder.

"Warm this up for me, Sam," I said.

"Cheapskate," Sam said in his usual charming way, "have a fresh cup on me. Why'd you let it get so cool?"

"I was talking to Frank in his cab, he has some silly ideas you know."

"You're joking," Sam handed me my coffee. "You haven't heard!"

"Heard what?"

"Frank died in his sleep two nights ago. He wasn't here. His cab wasn't here. You just stood over there for twenty minutes and let your coffee go cold. I was going to come over and see if you were OK."

"You're joshing me, Sam... and it's not funny."

"Honest, I ain't joshing you. Frank died two nights ago and that's that."

When I heard how earnest Sam's voice was, I shuddered. I drank my coffee as quickly as I could and thanked him.

"I'm gonna call it a night... there's not much doing anyway. Goodnight Sam."

Back in my cab I called despatch and asked about Frank. He was dead alright, the funeral was in three days' time.

I started the engine and turned onto the riverside road. I crossed a bridge and drove into the heart of the city. Mist was crawling into the streets and by the time day broke it would be a dull grey morning, but at least the rain had stopped.

As I twisted and turned through the old city centre towards home, I noticed alleyways, narrow streets, cuts and snickets I had never noticed before, their darkness was so dark, so solid, they were impossible to see into, but something about them called, a siren voice, a beating pulse, come to me, come to me. I managed to stay on the lighted streets, I managed not to turn into the welcoming blackness. Now I understood where Jonny Swiggert had gone... and the others I didn't know.

"I told you," Frank's voice said, "the old knowledge."

Shadow

Inebriates

Last night I took the riverside walk for the first time in longer than I care to remember. Nothing much had changed.

Homeless men and women were still spending the night on municipal benches. Some were asleep, they breathed noisily, or moaned. They looked like bundles of rags, although one or two of them had contrived to wrap flattened cardboard boxes around themselves. Others were awake, and clutched their most valuable possession close to them, a bottle of cheap wine or methylated spirits, in which they perhaps found escape or comfort or oblivion. They were all sickly, sicklier than they even knew. That's what came of inhaling the cold, damp air and autumn mist that visited them from the sluggish water. One by one they would die here, or somewhere else, it didn't really matter. That's the way it had always been.

As I passed these lost and abandoned people, I moved slowly, for I had no reason to hurry—on this or any other night. I would not be in this place for long, there were other places I would visit later, places that really suited me so much better.

I watched as a man just ahead of me struggled to his feet. He almost fell as he stood. Then he slumped down, in a sitting position, onto his bench again.

"Shadow," he said, his voice not quite a whisper, as I drew abreast of him. That's what they always called me. I don't know where the name came from, or what these unfortunates saw to make them believe I was a shadow.

I paused and looked at the man. No light reflected from his eyes, everything about him spoke of darkness. He said nothing more. He'd forgotten me, and was removing the screw-on cap from his bottle.

When I walked away, I heard that single word again, 'Shadow', as indistinct as a distant voice carried by a breeze. I turned and looked back to the man on the bench, he was now swigging from his bottle. Seeing how absorbed he was, in the only thing that gave his life meaning, I realised that he may not have spoken at all.

Five metres above my head, the street-lights on the parapet wall were wrapped in glaucomatous halos caused by the thin river mist. My silhouette was no longer visible by their light as it slid silently across the stone slabs beneath my feet. Only the creaking sounds of pleasure cruisers moored until the tourist season came again, and the gentle lapping of the river, found their way to my ears. At this time of the morning, near silence was always the most common sound in this part of the city. Farther away, fish and vegetable markets would be alive with activity as they prepared for the wholesale transactions that fed the street markets in every quarter. Here though, the city still slept, that's why I liked it, this was my time.

Shadows That Remain

I had left my atelier an hour earlier, and had allowed my feet to bring me here, as they threaded their way through the maze of forgotten alleys and snickets that are hidden by the modern stores and offices and apartment buildings that everyone knows. Along the way I'd passed the memories of people I knew well. There was the old lamplighter who knew nothing of electricity—the wonder of his time was gas—his shadow was still where he'd left it, visible only to those who knew where to look. Georgina, for such she called herself, although her real name, I'd heard, was Mavis Bloodworthy, still offered to perform any kind of sex act, with anybody, for a few pennies, enough to keep her in gin for an hour. "Quick fuck, love," I heard her say. My hand was feeling for coins in my pocket before I remembered she too was gone. Then I came upon little Robert, his was a story so sad it pained me as I recalled it, but still he smiled, and still he politely lifted his cap as I quickly passed him.

Gilbert Barnfeather

Then there was Gilbert Barnfeather. I had never encountered him but, like everyone of his time, I knew of him. He was reviled as a killer of dogs before he turned to killing people, and of those he had slaughtered fourteen, men, women and children—he had no preference, it was said that he simply enjoyed watching the life drain out of one of his fellows—before he was caught by officers of the law. I didn't attend his public hanging, believing it to be too bloodthirsty an event for my delicate disposition. Afterwards it was said that he hadn't died quickly, and that he was left hanging for days, his struggle for life slowly ending. Several months later, when I decided I could once again pass through the tiny square at the confluence of streets and alleyways where the gibbet had been erected, all that remained was the shadow of a man jerking and twisting on a wall. People were going about their business as usual, children were playing, dogs were barking. I accosted a person I knew vaguely, he was a trader in tobacco and I had, on occasion, purchased from him, I asked him about the shadow.

"Does it not make you shiver every time you pass it by?"

"No sir, it does not," he replied. "That foul person received the punishment he deserved, and his shadow will forever be there as a warning to other miscreants."

As he went on his way, I thought how abrupt his manner had been.

Barnfeather's shadow still dances on that wall when the sun shines brightly, and seeing it still chills me to the marrow.

That's one of the reasons I seldom walk by day, even though those alleys are often gloomy places. Most shadows that remain, especially when they are the shadows of those who lived without harming others, are visible by the light of streetlamps as well as sunshine, but Barnfeather's shadow, thankfully, needs the strongest of sunlight to give it life.

The Hall of Clocks

By and by I came upon the hall of clocks. This was not exactly a place of business, nor was it exactly a service for the benefit of the public. I think I can best describe it as an obsession that in some measure provides the gentleman—for indeed he is a gentleman—who is always in attendance with an income of sorts.

He is a man small of stature and thin of limb. His fingers are like the legs of a spider, and appear to be capable of acts of dexterity of which the fingers of a person such as myself are incapable. Residents of this ancient quarter bring him their clocks whenever they need his attention.

"Time has stopped," I heard an old woman say to him, on one very rainy evening, as she deposited a medium sized clock, that appeared, to me, to be of Germanic origin, in front of him.

"Oh no," the man said, "you see, madam, time never stops. Time, as measured by your beautiful clock, is simply taking a rest. It needs to be reawakened."

He then proceeded to open the hinged door on the back of the clock, and allowed his spindly fingers to crawl inside. I heard a pinging sound, followed by a metallic twang.

"There," he said, with an air of mild satisfaction as he closed the door. Turning the clock to face him he opened the glass front, and then fumbled with a large bunch of keys that were hanging from his belt. Finding the one he sought, he used it to carefully wind the clock's mechanism, one turn, two turns, three turns, and then set the hands to the correct time. By now the clock was healthily ticking

"With careful use your clock will last forever," he said to the woman. She smiled at him, dropped two or three into his hand, picked up her clock and left.

"What did you do to that clock, sir? How did you awaken the time within it?" I asked as my curiosity caused me to be imprudently curious.

"My fingers know," he said, "I permit them to enter a clock and they know what they must do. Can I be of assistance to you?"

"I have but come to admire your wonderful clocks." I spread my arms expansively to include the hundreds of clocks arrayed around us. "Such workmanship they display. But tell me sir, why are they all silent."

"Their times are resting," he replied, "all but for this one." He rested his hand on an elegant carriage-clock. "This one shows the time for today. Tomorrow another will show the correct time. That's how it must be."

I smiled at him.

"I have all of time here. Last year and next year and all the years that flow to and from them."

I felt some uncertainty as to what he meant, but I offered him no more questions. Instead, I pulled a few small value coins from my pocket and, as the old woman had done, I dropped them into the palm of his hand.

"Thank you," he said as I turned to leave, "please return whenever you feel the need."

Many times I have returned to visit him. He appears never to change. For myself, I find it most reassuring to know that time is in such good and capable hands.

Forgiveness

I must beg your forgiveness or, at the very least, your indulgence. For during my rambling discourse, which I had intended should take place only within my mind, I have become aware that others may be listening. If you are from that part of the city which we call the World of Haste, it is possible, indeed it is likely, that you are unaware not only of some of those things I have touched upon, such as the shadows that remain, but also of the very existence of our ancient places at the heart of what you consider to be your city. If this should be the case, if you continue to listen, you will, I hope, gain some understanding of the fact that our two societies have coexisted for many, many years. We frequently pass between our places and yours, you may have noticed us from time to time, you may have dismissed us as odd, but you seldom find your way to those places where we might congregate, such as the inns, or the chapagogue—indeed, perhaps I should speak of the chapagogue, since it will be quite unfamiliar to you if you are of the World of Haste.

The Chapagogue

There was a time when our city was one, by your way of measuring time that was several centuries ago, to us it was as yesterday. For reasons we choose not to remember, many people came to despise our Jewish citizens, and those times being less tolerant than today a pogrom came about. Those of our Jewish brethren who were not killed, fled to other places. Only the Rabbi remained, but so frightened was he of being killed that he forsook his faith and was baptised a Christian. He converted his synagogue into a church, and thereafter referred to it as the Church of the Cleansing. I knew this man, not as a close associate, but sufficiently well to be polite to him whenever we encountered each other. From the day of his conversion it was rumoured that his new faith was not founded in Biblical principles. In fact, he had become a convenient combination of Christian and Jew. Years later, when Jewish traders began to return to our city, he began to refer to his building as his 'chapagogue', for it served the needs of both faiths, who soon found that they could worship together in harmony. That situation abides to this day.

The World of Haste

With the hall of clocks and the chapagogue well behind me, I emerged from our city and entered the World of Haste on a wide boulevard that followed the course of the river. Even at this hour of the morning, when the pavements were empty of people and the road without its daytime throng of horseless carriages, bright street lights were still shining. I must say here that I so much prefer the more human glow of our gas lamps and tallow candles, because they do not create a sense of daylight when the world should be in darkness.

I made my way across the road, and thus it was I came to the steps that took me down to the riverside walk, where I passed slowly by the many resting indigent and inebriates and heard someone, I really know not whom, how could I possibly know, call me Shadow, in a whispered voice as I passed him by. I did not look at the man, of that I had no need, for I knew that like all those here, those who lived with the clinking of bottles, those who slept, when they slept, to the lapping of the river's waters against worn stone, that he was a discarded soul well beyond any help I might offer. When I was a step or two beyond him, I heard a deep sigh that rattled with the sound of life trying to escape a dying body. I had often heard it whispered among these sad people, that the touch of my shadow, my very passing, pulled life away from those willing to give it leave to depart from them. How could that be, especially here, where on a night such as this shadows, including my own shadow, were no more than gestures to the darkness.

Shadow was not my name of course, but it is what many of the unfortunates here have called me these several centuries past. Perhaps it is that any brethren from our city who choose to visit here are also called Shadow. In my city, our city, I have a name, but never will it be known to the World of Haste, as such passing of knowledge is forbidden to us.

I walked slowly along the riverside, catching the aroma of stagnant water as it rose up and dropped away again, sensing the life and death with which it was redolent. In the World of Haste, the river was cleaner than it had been through all the years I had known it, but it was not really clean, and I could well imagine the cargo of misery that travelled amongst its ripples, until it dropped to the river's bed and became the silt of life.

By and by as I walked, the river entered a large garden whose trees and shrubs came almost to the water's edge. How do I know this? Because long ago, perhaps as much as a century before this time, I often visited this city when the sun was upon the sky. I walked here by the light of day, I saw the seasons in this garden, from the glorious colours of summertime, to the dull greys and browns of winter. That was before the time of horseless carriages and shining birds that soared noisily across the sky, it was, in fact, before this World of Haste had come to pass. In that time, as I walked here, people would look at me with some curiosity, they would shake their heads, as if they were unsure as to whether they had seen me or not, then they would look right through me and go on their way, sometimes glancing back at me, sometimes not. I often wondered what thoughts had passed through their minds, whether they wanted to reach out and touch me to discover whether or not I was real.

Nowadays, the World of Haste, during the hours of daylight, is no place for anyone from our city.

Going Home

When I became aware that light was touching the Eastern rim of the sky, that the first moments of dawn were glinting from polished glass windows, I knew I had to leave the World of Haste. I had walked right through the garden, and had emerged close to the arches of a bridge across the river. I could remember the time before that bridge had been built, when this crossing had provided a living for a ferryman and his family. Now, the bridge arched slightly towards the tall buildings across the river, and though quiet now, it would soon teem with the people of this city and their omnibuses and horseless carriages.

Six hours, I estimated, I had been in this city, as I crossed the boulevard towards where I must go, that was time enough, and I would not feel the need to return here for many a long night.

As I approached the side street that would lead me back, by twists and turns, to the timeless streets and alleyways of our city, a young man approached me.

"You been to a fancy dress?" He asked.

"A fancy dress?" I asked him, unsure of what he meant, but I knew he would not hear me.

He reached out a hand to touch me. I felt it enter me, disrupt me. Then the man stumbled and fell to the ground, thrown off his balance by my incorporeality.

"What the…" I heard him call out, but by then I was around the corner of the street and approaching the snicket that the people from our city knew was there.

By the time I was threading my way through the maze of streets that led to my home, I could already hear the sounds of the World of Haste rising above the near silence in which I was.

Mr LaFarge and Mrs Mellow and Mr Bray

As I neared my street, I passed the apothecary's shop, I passed the bootmaker's, I passed the butcher's from where my nose detected the metallic tang of fresh blood. I came to the printery, where unfolded sheets of the *City Journal* were pegged on lines of thin string while their ink dried.

"A morning paper Mr ————?" The printer asked from the doorway.

"Alas, I have no coinage with me," I replied.

"That's quite alright sir, you may make good your small debt to me on the next occasion that you pass this way." With those kind words, he removed a copy of his publication from a small pile of dried and folded copies and handed it to me.

"Thank you most kindly, Mr LaFarge," I said, then I smiled and went on my way.

Freshly baked bread has, for me, always had a most enticing aroma, so a little nearer my atelier I paused outside Mrs Mellow's bakery shop, and looked longingly at the stack of freshly baked loaves in its window. Seeing me, Mrs Mellow, who made the most delicious bread, and who looked dumpling-like, just as a baker should, bustled out to greet me.

"All fresh this very morning, Mr ————," she said, "I've been working since three o'clock so you can enjoy your breakfast."

"Alas, I have no coinage with me," I said to her.

"That's quite alright Mr ————, you may make good your debt to me on the next occasion that you pass this way to buy my bread." With those kind words, she took a loaf, wrapped it in muslin and handed it to me.

"Thank you most kindly, Mrs Mellow," I said, then I smiled and went on my way.

By the time I reached the door to my atelier, I had already broken several morsels from Mrs Mellow's warm loaf to satisfy a hunger that I didn't know was there.

As I removed my key from a pocket, I heard a familiar voice.

"Milk sir? Fresh milk Mr ————?" Mr Bray asked.

"Yes indeed, Mr Bray," I replied. "I shall fetch a ewer that you may fill it for me."

I returned a moment tater, and watched as Mr Bray measured out my milk.

"I would like a good pat of butter too, if you please, to go with Mrs Mellow's fresh bread."

"And very fine bread it is Mr ————, very fine bread. That will be one groat, sir."

Having collected coins in my atelier, I made good my debt to Mr Bray.

"What a beautiful day it's going be, do you not think Mr Bray?"

He shrugged his shoulders. We both looked up at the sky, heard the distant noise of a metallic bird passing overhead.

"I do believe you may be right, Mr ————, good days in our city are always good days."

"Thank you Mr Bray, thank you," I said as I smiled, shook his hand, and went indoors to breakfast.

Five

Ghosts

A skein of migrating birds swerved and dipped across the grey winter sky, they were late this year but autumn was late and winter was late too. Although it was Christmas eve a few trees were still shedding summer's leaves. They drifted dry and brittle to the ground, where they crunched noisily beneath the man's feet as he walked homewards.

As he exhaled, his breath hung in cold, momentary clouds before him. He'd never understood where those clouds went, they were there, they were gone, that was all.

He hated Christmas. In fact he'd hated Christmas since he was a teenager, all the forced bonhomie, even when times were bad, the useless gifts and the feigned appreciation that followed their giving, the cold Christmas dinner, always cold because it was such a performance to prepare and cook in a small, outdated kitchen. He hated Christmas. He hated Christmas.

There was one particular thing about Christmas day he'd always dreaded above everything else. After the guests had gone, after the washing up was done and the leftover food stowed away, it was late and he was sent to bed. His parents wanted to drink, they didn't want him to see how much they would drink, but he knew, he knew. With each glass of sherry or whisky or beer they downed their voices became more vociferous, their insults one to the other more cruel. Christmas night always ended with doors slamming, his mother crying, his father hurling one final abusive tirade as she walked away. It wasn't a joyful time. There was no peace on earth and goodwill to all men in his home.

He was an only child and had no one to share his Christmas with. Friends were busy with their families, mostly happier families, and couldn't be with him until the two terrible days were over. His parents always argued, his mother always cried, but at Christmas, when his father was off work for a few days it was especially bad.

"I only stay with him for your sake dear," she said, and then, "I'm sorry, I didn't mean that."

She had meant it of course and the repressed tears that sparkled in her eyes proved that she had. The guilt for her situation was his. It was a heavy burden to carry.

Breakfast the next morning was a time of stolid silence and resentful glances that he was not meant to notice. As the morning progressed though, the silence between his parents turned into taciturn questions and curt responses, an improvement at least. It was always like that.

He was fourteen years old. Feeling quite daring he'd once asked his father why he and his mother didn't love each other anymore. Anger flashed in his father's eyes, but his words were gentle.

"We do love each other son, we really do. It's just that sometimes we don't see eye to eye, or your mother does something that makes me cross, and then we argue. We try to keep our problems from you, but. . ." His father's voice trailed to silence.

"You drink too much. It makes you angry."

After that the red mark of his father's hand was visible on his left cheek for hours, it was hot, it stung and the violence was seared into his soul. His father was capable of making him cry too.

That was the first violent outburst from his father that he could remember, but they grew in number and were directed mostly at his mother. He never saw his father strike her, but the mysterious bruises on arms and face, from walking into doors she said, showed more and more frequently.

"You should leave him mum, you should leave him." He said to her when he was sixteen.

"It will be alright dear," she said. "We'll work things out."

She stayed with his father until the day she died.

When he finally left home to go to college he felt a great sense of relief. He still worried about his mother. He 'phoned her several times a week, they laughed together, joked. Things were never less than alright, sometimes she was even happy she said, things were good. His father rarely wanted to speak to him, he was always busy, he would call him back, but he never did.

Christmases came and went and for the whole of his time at college and for several years after he'd graduated he found reasons not to go home. Finally it was a duty he could avoid no longer.

He walked reluctantly from the railway station to his parents' home on an edge of town estate. With him he had a small backpack containing a change of clothes, his toiletries and token gifts for his parents. Snow had fallen early that year, it was slippery underfoot. He could have taken a taxi from the station, but that would have been too quick, he was in no hurry to arrive. It was dark, and he wanted it to be darker to match his mood.

As he walked he occasionally passed others, no one called out 'hello' or 'merry Christmas' or acknowledged his presence at all. Anonymity was good. Where street lights cast shadows he lingered in them for as long as he could, feeling comfortable, as if he belonged there. Finally though, he had to move on.

He couldn't remember how long ago that first adult visit was or for how many years he'd made this Christmas visit now, but here he was again. The winter season changed from year to year, snowy, wet, windy, once almost balmy, this year noisy autumn leaves still on the ground, but nothing else changed. Unhappy ghosts from his childhood always haunted his memories, gave him a deep sense of foreboding. He sorrowed for his mother, despised his father more. Every year he decided there was no point being here, but on Christmas eve he always felt compelled to make the journey.

He reached the door of his parents' house, rang the bell, waited.

"Don't open the door, you know there'll be nobody there," he heard his father shout out.

"But maybe this year. . ."

"It's always the bloody same," anger in the voice, so much anger, "it's just the neighbourhood kids making trouble."

"He might not be dead, he might not be."

"Silly bitch, it was a train crash, thirty died, your son was one of them."

He'd heard the exchange many times. His father thought he was dead, his mother hoped. He didn't believe he was dead. How could that be? Here he was! He could feel, he could hear, he felt love for his mother in him.

The living room curtain twitched, he saw his mother's small face peer out. She looked so old.

"You're right," she sighed, "there's no one there."

He rang the doorbell once more, but the door didn't open. The door was never opened.

The Gift

Outside the sun was shining among clouds that threatened snow. Patches of blue sky were bright and welcoming. It was that time of year again.

Sally Grainger carefully slid the artificial Christmas tree from its long cardboard tube. It was the same tree they'd purchased thirty years earlier. It had lasted well. In the early afternoon light of Christmas eve the tree reflected silver and green. She pushed the stem of the tree into its tripod shaped plastic stand and then placed it in the corner of the room where it always went.

The box of festive baubles was in Tom's room and when she had fetched them from beneath her son's bed she took them to the kitchen and carefully removed the dust from each of them. She then returned with them to the tree. As she folded the tree branches out they shed flakes of tinsel that glistened as they twisted and turned, dancing their way to the floor. Soon she was doing what she enjoyed most about getting ready for Christmas. It took her forty minutes to place the baubles where she wanted them to be.

Sally stood back and admired her work. Although they would have no other decorations for Christmas, although they had received not a single Christmas card, the room looked very festive. The tree was beautiful and the mirrored balls of silver, gold, blue, red, moved gently upon it, as if being lightly caressed by hands she couldn't see. Everything was right for her.

******

When Peter came home he hugged his wife.

"The tree looks lovely Mrs G," he said. "You always do it so well, so nicely."

Sally smiled at him. He'd said the same thing to her every Christmas eve for thirty years.

"It's very cold out there. It might snow, you know."

He said that every Christmas eve as well. These banalities were a ritual, words they were both comfortable with.

"I'll go and make dinner," Sally said, "it's nothing special."

"That's all right dear; I'm so hungry I could eat anything."

More familiar words, but their familiarity didn't bother Sally.

They had been married for thirty-one years and were a good match. Peter was the breadwinner. He earned a modest salary doing a modest job that he'd done to the best of his ability since before they'd met. They lived within their means, never borrowed, never used credit. They even had a small amount of money in the bank. Every year they talked about taking a holiday, somewhere nice, but they never did.

Sally was a dutiful housewife, it fulfilled her. She took pleasure from dusting and washing and ironing and keeping everything neat. She knew she was supposed to want more than this in the modern world, but she was satisfied with what she had and she enjoyed looking after Peter.

******

After dinner they sat and talked for a few minutes. They didn't talk about anything important. They had no real interests apart from their life together. In fact, if someone had walked in and asked them what they were talking about neither of them would have remembered. Their empty plates were still before them, the bottle of cheap white wine was still half full after their one careful glass each.

"I'll go and do the dishes now," Sally said as she pushed the cork back into the neck of the wine bottle. "If you want more wine you know where it will be."

Peter never wanted more wine.

As he walked from the kitchen to the living room Peter decided it was time to wrap the gift.

"You should wrap the gift now," Sally called out, echoing his thoughts.

In Tom's room he pulled the large and brightly coloured box from beneath the bed. Through the transparent plastic window in its lid he admired the collection of die-cast toy cars. They were all models from thirty years ago of course.

There was wrapping paper left from last year, it was covered with images of teddy bears and Santa Claus.

Five minutes later the gift was wrapped in a way that any child would love.

******

"There's nothing on worth watching." There was never anything worth watching on TV according to Peter, but they watched a lot anyway.

Every now and then, as the evening passed, they would gaze at the Christmas tree.

"It looks lovely."

"Yes it does."

"You did well this year."

"Thank you. I like it."

When the TV news came on at ten o'clock Peter reached for the remote control and switched their set to standby.

"It's time," he said. "I'll get the gift."

"I'll light the candles."

Sally lit the candles, two in the window, one each side of the gas fire, each in a shaped glass jar, just as she had done for the last thirty years. Peter returned and carefully placed the gift beneath the tree.

"I'll move our chairs closer together." He said.

"I'll get the sherry and mince pies."

She'd prepared a tray earlier. Two glasses. Six supermarket mince pies on a plate. A bottle of no-brand sherry she had already opened. She set the tray on the low table between their chairs.

"That all looks grand," Peter said.

"The light, will you do the honours?" Sally asked as she seated herself and felt the comforting warmth from the gas fire reach her.

It was part of their ritual. It was what they always did, a sedate duty dance to mark something they didn't understand. To them it seemed to be the right thing to do and so they had followed their Christmas eve ritual for thirty years.

Candles flickered, gas fire glowed, and with the room light off still gave enough light to see all they needed to see.

Minutes passed.

As one they each stretched an arm across the table and took the other's hand.

"Your hand, your skin is so soft," Peter said quietly.

"And your hand is an honest hand, the hand of a man who has done his best all his life."

Each gave the other's hand a gentle, loving squeeze and then relinquished their hold.

Minutes passed.

As one they reached down to the tray. Peter poured sherry. Sally lifted the plate of mince pies.

"Sherry Mrs G," Peter said.

"Mince pie Mr G," Sally said.

Minutes passed.

They sipped their sherry in a genteel way, carefully ate their mince pies.

Minutes passed.

"I think it's almost time Mr G," Sally said.

"I think you're right Mrs G." Peter replied.

Minutes passed.

They stared at the tree, watching, waiting, just as they had done for thirty years. In the silent room the only sounds they could hear were the gentle pop-pop-pop of candle flames, the soft hiss of the gas fire and their own shallow, expectant breathing.

Minutes passed.

"I think we have a visitor, Mrs G." Peter whispered.

"I think we have Mr. G."

As Peter and Sally watched, the gift slid from beneath the Christmas tree—the tree shaking so much they thought it might topple—then it rose into the air to a height of about two feet, turned on its side and jiggled about as if being shaken, the toys inside rattling audibly. When it returned to the carpeted floor a flurry of tearing sounds followed as the wrapping paper was eagerly ripped away. Ever hopeful they waited to hear a squeal of delight, an acknowledgement, a sigh, sounds they had wanted to hear for thirty years, but no such sounds came.

They sat motionless, silent, as events took their course. They were holding hands again, gripping each other hard.

Toy cars were now lined up on the carpet in order of size, then they shifted around until ordered by colour. One by one the cars moved across the floor, some just a few feet in one direction or another, others much closer to where they were sitting.

Peter and Sally watched and watched, trying to remember if this car or that was making the same moves this year as it had last year and the year before that, but they couldn't remember. A few years earlier Peter had tried to record these events using his cell phone; in the low light it hadn't worked and Sally was glad. Some things were meant to be seen and felt but not kept forever.

They had never measured how long their visitor stayed, but when one by one the toy cars stopped moving they knew their Christmas eve was almost over.

"It's finished," Peter said eventually. "Our visitor came again."

Although they were still curious they had long ago agreed that they would not try to understand, to define or put a name to what they were experiencing. Inwardly though, they had both decided what this was, and if they had discussed it they would have been aware that they both thought the same.

"Yes, it's finished," Sally agreed, "until next Christmas."

"Time for bed Mrs G."

"Yes, let's go to bed Mr G."

******

In each others arms they were comfortable and warm. There was no suggestion of sex. They hadn't had sex on Christmas eve for thirty years. They slept soundly, only shifting their positions slightly as night moved towards day. A few hours later they woke up together, still in each other's arms.

Sally had dreamed a bad dream, just as she had for the last thirty years, but it hadn't made her restless, it was an old dream now. She was walking towards the supermarket, to buy Christmas food, pushing her three year old son in his buggy. A delivery van, it's horn blaring and brakes screeching, mounted the pavement, swept her buggy from her hands and crushed it against a brick wall. She screamed over and over and when she could scream no more she cried and sobbed. Through her tears she could see the remains of her son's twisted buggy merged with the Transit van. Beneath the wreck, engine oil, petrol and blood swirled together. The van's driver was bleeding heavily, his blood dripping into the pool below.

"Good morning Mr G," Sally said. | She couldn't remember her dream but had a sadness about her.

"Good morning Mrs G."

They jumped out of bed together, washed one after the other, dressed and went to the kitchen together.

In the living room toy cars and wrapping paper were littered across the floor, sherry and mince pies were still between their chairs.

"You pack the gift away and take the tree down," Sally said. "I'll make breakfast."

"I will," Peter sighed. "That's Christmas over for another year."

"Yes, that's Christmas over for another year," Sally said wistfully.

Then they both went about their appointed tasks, busy, unthinking, just as they had done for the last thirty years.

The Darkness

When people talk about the Darkness they don't really understand. They laugh about it, they joke about it, they brush all mention of it aside as if it's nothing. It's something they've heard about or read about in the sensationalist press. It's not real. It's not to be taken seriously. When it crops up in conversation only those who have experienced the Darkness refrain from voicing an opinion and stay silent, so I know who they are.

There are other ways in which I know who they are as well.

It doesn't matter where I am—in my office, in the metro, in a store, at a party—those who know the Darkness wear their knowledge like a badge that only others like them can see. They have a quietness about them, a reluctance to smile, to laugh. Their eyes are downcast, they want to be invisible. They take frequent small glances behind them, peer through open doors before crossing the threshold. If they can, they make detours around large shadows, if they can't they quicken their pace—and hope. If their eyes chance to meet those of another like them, they quickly look away, but each has already shared their pity for the other. This is what they are like in public places; in private I know they will be just the same as I am.

I never used to be a fearful man. Ebullience was second nature to me. I was a joker, the one who made light of even the most serious situation.

Friends sometimes found my constant cheerfulness tiresome. In a way that pleased me. I wanted them to be more like me, they told me to act my age, whatever that meant. Colleagues felt the same about me and even my boss had quietly told me that work was not the place for a frivolous attitude. To my mind the problem was theirs, not mine.

"Get real," I said on more than one occasion, "none of this really matters."

"It might not matter to you, but it matters to me." Was the usual rejoinder, the 'it' being anything from a sales analysis spreadsheet to problems with a girlfriend or car.

Then my life changed.

Home was a couple of miles away, a small apartment in a ten storey block. The office Christmas party had died. People had left and only the die-hard drinkers remained, determined to squeeze every free drink they could from the company's bank account. I wasn't in their league, even though I enjoyed good Scotch—preferably an aged and peaty single malt. I made my way to the door of the small drinking club we'd taken over for the night, called out my farewells and stepped outside. No one seemed to notice that I was leaving, there was no chorus of goodnights, no imploring me to have one more for the road. I was glad about that, because I hated long goodbyes—you know, those that drag out for half an hour or more because no one really wants to end it.

Chill December air washed over me. I pulled my coat around me and buttoned it, leaving only the top button undone. I'd already decided to walk home, reasoning that it would help clear my head for whatever I had to do when morning came— not when tomorrow came, as it was past midnight already—the first day of the Christmas break.

I headed across the road and turned right towards the river that meanders through the city. A cyclist zipped past me purposefully, hell-bent on an early-hours errand urgent only to him. Occasional cars crept along, their drivers drawing attention to themselves by moving so slowly along a quiet street, probably convinced that by doing so any police on duty wouldn't realise they'd had too much to drink. As I neared the junction with the riverside road I could see the two strings of lights on the parapets of the bridge diminishing towards the far side of the river.

Whenever I walked to or from my office I crossed this bridge. Usually it was crowded with traffic and thronged with pedestrians hurrying, hurrying, lost to those around them, no good mornings no good evenings, just cold shouldered silence. Now the bridge was empty, no plodding feet, no purring engines no impatient hammering on car horns. A cold breeze was blowing off the river and from down below I could hear the insistent lapping of water against stone piers. Here and there patches of mist swirled, but they were nothing compared to the thick fog that sometimes rises here. All in all it was a good December night.

I heard the sound of a diesel engine and a car drew alongside me pacing my slow walk.

"Cab sir?" The driver asked through his open window. "It's late you know."

"I don't have far to go now, I'll keep walking thanks." I smiled at him as I spoke, but I doubt that he noticed as he pulled away. There were no markings on the vehicle, no illuminated sign, unlicensed obviously.

Approaching the mid point of the bridge I was almost half way home. This is a low city, with few buildings more than fifteen storeys high, on my side of the river my apartment block is one of the tallest buildings around. I could see its silhouette against the night sky, a large, dark obelisk studded with occasional lights. As the crow flies it was about half a mile away, but walking I still had a mile to go.

Behind me I heard the slap of running feet, a voice calling indistinct words. I expected to see no one at this hour, but when I turned to look I saw someone running towards me, passing in and out of the glowing cones cast by the bridge lights.

"Are you OK?" I called out when the figure—still of indeterminate gender—was close enough to hear.

The sound that came back to me, quite clear despite the sound of the river and the noise of running feet, was like the mewling of a baby but deeper, harsher.

"Are you OK?" I called again.

This time the response was louder, it sounded angry and didn't stop. At that point I gave up and resumed my walk. An offer of concern doesn't have to be welcomed or accepted. I'd done what anyone would have done and my conscience was clear.

A few steps farther on and I knew the person was right behind me, but the urgent footfall didn't falter, didn't slow. Whoever this was they were in a hurry to be somewhere.

I have no explanation for what happened in the next few minutes, all I can do is tell you as much as I remember.

I felt what I assume to be the running figure brush against me, or that's what it felt like at first. It made contact with me anyway. Then something was all around me, it was as though I was in a mist, but I could still see the bridge, the lights, the distant buildings as clearly as I had since I'd left the party. At the same time a numbing coldness filled me, not a cold like a winter night, something deeper and colder that chilled me in a way that I now call 'the cold chill of fear'. Both the chill and the sense of mistiness left me very quickly, but they left me shivering and standing motionless against the stone parapet. Ahead of me the running figure reappeared, consolidating itself out of the December air and I felt that I was attached to it, almost as if something of me had been pulled out with that deep, deep cold.

As I watched, the figure. . . oozed—it's the best word I have—up onto the parapet and flowed down into the river below. It was gone.

As I resumed walking, still shivering violently, I thought about looking down into the water, but it was dark. . . and my nerve had left me. When I neared the spot where the figure had entered the river I heard wave after wave of deep sighing sounds, that were more sad and despairing than frightening; but I pulled away from the parapet anyway. I wanted to offer help, to cry—but offer help to what? Cry about what? Instead I tried to quicken my pace, but my feet felt as though they were walking through something viscous and insistent. When I looked down darkness darker than the night had oozed over my shoes and was inching up the legs of my jeans. I couldn't feel it on me, but it was there. I tried to run, but that was useless.

"Are you ready for a cab now sir? It might be a good idea. I'll help you into the back."

It was the same friendly voice, the same unmarked cab that I'd refused a short while ago. The driver opened the rear door, took my arm and guided me onto the seat. My feet were free, there was no darkness enveloping my legs.

"Saw you about two hours ago not far from here. Had one too many have we? I hope you wasn't thinking about jumping, seen that before I have."

A few minutes later and I'd paid the driver the rather high fare he'd asked for and was unlocking my apartment door.

I can't explain what happened. Don't tell me I imagined it, because I didn't. It happened.

What's more it left something with me.

Every time I go out in the darkness, every time I step into a daytime shadow, no matter where it is, I look down and see that despairing darkness on my shoes again, creeping up my legs, threatening to engulf me and claim what it owns. That's why my friends ask what's happened to me. That's why my eyes are downcast, why I want to be invisible. That's why I glance behind myself so often, peer through open doors before crossing the threshold and make detours around large shadows.

What's more, it's my company's Christmas party tomorrow night and guess what, I won't be going.

Japy

Click. Clickety-Clack. Click. Clack. Ping. Zrrrrrrrrrph. Thunk. Click. Clickety-Clack. Click. Clack. Ping. Zrrrrrrrrrph. Thunk.

Sabine came awake slowly. The sounds impinging on her semi-sleeping mind both harsh and familiar. Her high-ceilinged bedroom was cold, a December breeze lifting the curtain allowed occasional flashes of light from the street lamp outside her window to throw the room momentarily into stark visibility. Hard, dark shadows, patches of equally hard-edged light, made everything unfamiliar. She had heard the sounds before, but couldn't identify them and now they had stopped. Not alert enough to be concerned, she turned her back to the window, pulled her bedcovers around her and went back to sleep.

Click. Clickety-Clack. Click. Clack. Ping. Zrrrrrrrrrph. Thunk.
Click. Clickety-Clack. Click. Clack. Ping. Zrrrrrrrrrph. Thunk.

That noise again. She had no memory of waking up earlier. She looked at her alarm clock, its luminous hands showed just after four a.m. It wasn't time to get up yet. There was no RER journey into central Paris to undertake, no dash through almost empty streets to the office, in fact it was going to be a lazy day. She stretched her limbs, snuggled down and slept again.

It was a fitful sleep. She dreamed of her grandfather and imagined that he had become a great novelist instead of a journeyman writer working mostly to assignments. He'd written several novels that no one remembered, but she thought they were good and re-read them every few years. She could précis their stories for anyone without reference to the books. She dreamed happy dreams of her children, all adults now with lives of their own. Memories of her husband came into those dreams, but she had seldom seen him since their marriage had ended; he was a ghost that existed only inside her. She dreamed of people whose names she didn't know, shadowy people she saw on the metro and narrow back streets of Paris, always enigmatic and never quite real to her, their lives waiting to be written.

Somehow another four hours passed, she tossed and turned, the room grew lighter. A noisy street sweeper went by and she awoke again. People passed, chattering noisily. None of her dreams were remembered. She did recall the strange night-time sounds though, and decided they were more a nuisance than something to worry about.

As she walked into her living-room she was surprised at how untidy she had left it, normally she was fastidious. The evening of the third day of Christmas had been a private time. She had relaxed, eaten lightly and drunk several glasses of Pinot Noir. She had played her favourite music more loudly than her neighbours in this old apartment block would have liked, but she owed them that. She had sung along to the songs she loved; she had danced with her shadow remembering the dancing of her youth. Finally she had relaxed on her engulfing sofa and fallen asleep until a ping from her mobile 'phone woke her and she muttered "I'm tired. Bonne nuit world." It had been a good evening.

Her day passed doing essential things, necessary things, things that pleased her. She bought flowers from a street-seller, visited her favourite boulangerie, bought aromatic candles and small treats for herself. When the shopping was done, she returned home, made tea and sipped it slowly. Then it was out again for a stroll in the nearby park before darkness claimed the day.

Sunshine streamed through scattered clouds in the bluest of blue winter skies, the fragrance of winter flowers was everywhere in the cold air. Parents played with their children, old folk stuttered along just happy to have seen another Christmas. Even the ice-cream seller was doing a busy trade.

It was days like this that Sabine appreciated most, when the troubles of others were being kept from her and her own troubles and troubled memories were not hurting or haunting her too much. There was terrible sadness in her recent past, but she was dealing with it and today had been a good day.

That evening after eating and enjoying a single glass of Pinot Noir she caught a movie on TV, an old musical that she could watch forever—never mind its simple story, its idealised romance and perfect people—it was the songs she loved. As usual she fell asleep. She awoke to the discordant opening music of a political discussion show, turned her television off and went to bed.

Click. Clickety-Clack. Click. Clack. Ping. Zrrrrrrrrrph. Thunk. Click. Clickety-Clack. Click. Clack. Ping. Zrrrrrrrrrph. Thunk.

In the early hours the sounds woke her again. She wearily ignored the noise and went back to sleep. That night it happened twice more, and her last few hours of sleep were fretful and disturbed.

In the morning she was for the first time concerned about the night-time noises and while taking her breakfast she wondered what she could do. They had been occurring for more than a week now, two times, three times, one night four times, but not missing a night. She wasn't even sure whether the sounds originated in her apartment or somewhere in the street outside, but she knew she would have to find out.

Click. Clickety-Clack. Click. Clack. Ping. Zrrrrrrrrrph. Thunk. Click. Clickety-Clack. Click. Clack. Ping. Zrrrrrrrrrph. Thunk.

Her sleep was shallow. Turning on her bedside light read the note—large letters on an unruled sheet—she'd left herself. 'Listen for where the noise comes from!'

She did as she was told, sat on the side of her bed and listened, listened. She cocked her head towards the open window, then to her closed bedroom door. There was no moment of epiphany, just a slow realization that it was a familiar sound, one she hadn't heard for many years—and it was coming from inside her apartment. She knew what it was and she wasn't afraid, only puzzled.

She entered her living room, turned on the light. Her grandfather's ancient Japy typewriter lived dustily on the bottom shelf of her bookcase. Its keys were being struck by an invisible force over and over again. The typebars rising and hitting the platen. The end of line bell pinging. The carriage return lever swung inwards, the carriage sliding noisily to the right, a new line starting. She watched in fascination, trying to discern whether there was any pattern to the striking of the keys, but if there was, she was too tired to notice.

Realizing that she should have been at least a little frightened, she smiled and thought of her grandfather.

Sabine, Sabine, don't you dream
Of monsters in the night;
Dream instead of the fairy queen
And gentle morning light.

Those were the words her grandfather used to chant to her when as a child she awoke from a bad dream; she was always soothed as his gentle voice, repeating the words over and over, lulled her back to the rhythms of sleep.

"Grandpapa was so good with you when he was alive," her mother had often reminded her. "When you were a little one you would sleep for him like you would sleep for no one else."

How could she be afraid now?

Switching off the light, closing her bedroom door behind her, she returned to her bed. The clatter of the typewriter didn't stop, but it didn't concern her any more and she slept.

Her curiosity got the better of her the next night and she wound a sheet of paper into the typewriter. She wanted so much to know what was being typed, but even as the keys rattled in the night she kept herself from looking until the following morning.

****

```
This is the story of my life.
    It was a life of magic and joy, terror and pain,
but not always in ways that you will recognise.
    I remember the moment of my birth.
    I remember the moment of my death.
    I remember every second of every day of every
week of every year that I lived.
    Impossible! Impossible! I can hear you protesting
already, but my words are the truth. It might be
that my truth is not the same as your truth but truth
it is, because truth is relative to the person we
are, the child we were and the person we eventually
become.
    Read with an open mind, do not judge me, and I
will tell you all about my life.
```

****

There was more. It seemed impossible to her that a single sheet could tell so much and yet tell so little.

Her grandfather had died when she was young and her memories of him were vague. Her mother had told her about him, but she was speaking as a daughter and duty and love always colour truth. Now her grandfather was speaking directly to her and that night she put paper into the typewriter before she went to bed. She slept soundly, heard no night-time noise, but next morning she had another six-hundred words to read.

Winding paper into the typewriter became part of her routine, every time she left her apartment, each night when she went to bed, she made certain that the typewriter was ready for use. She never questioned this. Each morning, every time she returned home, there was a new episode to make her laugh, to make her cry, to make her wonder. Never again was she disturbed by the rapid typing, but over the months that followed, two sheets became three-hundred sheets, four hundred sheets and then seven-hundred sheets. How the inked ribbon of the Japy had lasted so long and so well she didn't know, it was just one impossibility amongst many.

Then it was over. It was almost Christmas again and on a bright morning she removed the sheet of paper from behind the retaining fingers and it held only a few dozen words.

****

```
    . . . saw the Tsar again after that. I learned
that he and his beautiful family had been disposed
of by the Bolsheviks in a most cruel manner.
    I escaped Russia, crossing on foot to Estonia,
thence to Finland and finally to Paris, the great
city where I made my life—but you already know of
that.
    You will have many questions I am sure, but
the answers are all in my story, you only have to
decide what those answers are. The events of my
life, the years in which they took place, the days
of my birth and death you can order in any way that
pleases you, just as I have ordered them in the way
that most pleases me.
    Sabine, Sabine, don't you dream
    Of monsters in the night;
    Dream instead of the fairy queen
    And gentle morning light.
    Goodbye.
```

****

When she finished reading those final words she wiped a single tear from the corner of her eye. Without realising it she sighed several times.

She kept paper in the Japy for months after that, hoping, always hoping, but her grandfather never spoke to her again.

Armand

Early January, cold, grey, soft snow underfoot. Isabelle C——— made her way back to the one-roomed schoolhouse dreading her first day in her new job. Her morning walk had cleared her head after a little too much wine last night.

****

She'd left behind her hectic life in Paris, her expensive apartment—so small, but the best she could afford on her teacher's salary—and was determined to make a new life for herself in a place where the clocks ticked more slowly.

A day or two before Christmas she had arrived at Montrésor, a village so small it barely existed. She'd parked her car in the village square, walked the tight, cobbled streets among houses of timber and stone, their summer flower-baskets dark and dead. She stared at the chateau, the church, the ruined castle that towered over the low huddle of buildings. She saw no one.

She made her way to a café-bar, perhaps the only one in the village, and ordered coffee.

Old men fell silent as she entered, stared at her, their dominos still, their flat beers forgotten. Bars such as this were the haunts of old men, they came for the warmth of the blazing log fire, the company of other lonely, forgotten people like themselves. A small glass of beer took hours to drink. They talked noisily, slammed their dominos onto the table-top, became irritable when someone outplayed them and looked suspiciously on strangers. When their conversation returned, they whispered secrets Isabelle could not hear.

She turned towards them, smiled.

"Bonjour," she said.

Their cold stares turned to grins, their wrinkled mouths displaying isolated, tombstone teeth.

"Bonjour," they said, one by one.

Then dominos rattled again and they talked loudly and with the garrulous enthusiasm of those who know that their time to spend words might soon be over. She was no longer a stranger.

She sipped her strong, dark coffee and gratefully ate the single caramelised biscuit that came with it—there was a hint of cinnamon too she thought.

"You are passing through?" The barman asked.

"No," Isabelle replied, "I will live here."

"But no one new comes to Montrésor, people only move away."

"I will be the new teacher at your school."

"C'est bien ! Monsieur Benoit has retired. He was our teacher for many years. I was his élévè once and now I am almost old."

Isabelle smiled.

"No monsieur, you are not old."

She asked him for directions to the mayorie, paid for her coffee and was about to leave.

"The mayorie will not be open mademoiselle."

"When will it be open monsieur."

"No more today. That is our mayor playing dominos." He pointed to a man who might well have been the youngest of the four and called out his name. "Our new teacher. She has arrived."

****

He finished his beer and reluctantly left his dominos. He walked with her to the schoolhouse, unlocked the door and entered with her. The school-room was shabby, everything was old. He noticed the look of disappointment on her face.

"This is a poor community, there is no money for new things Mademoiselle C——." He spread his arms, shrugged his shoulders in the way typical of his countrymen. "Your rooms are through that door, you will find them better than this. M. Benoit was a fastidious man."

She took the key from him as he left.

"You are in charge now mademoiselle."

He was right about her accommodation, it was compact but provided everything she would need. The few personal things she had brought with her would soon make this her home and more would come from Paris little by little.

****

She unlocked the door of the schoolroom and stamped snow from her boots before she entered. Yesterday, even though it was Sunday, a man had come to show Isabelle how to use the electric heating system, so inside it was warm.

Pencils were sharpened, text books set out, and in ones and two her class of six and seven year olds trooped into the room.

"Bonjour maîtresse. Bonjour maîtresse. "Bonjour maîtresse."

She answered their small, bright voices with eighteen 'bonjours' and eighteen smiles.

Seated before her they chattered amongst themselves, some were known to one another, some were making new friends, one or two showed no excitement and cried quietly in this unfamiliar environment.

"Silence!!" She called out loud enough to be heard above the noise of the children. When they were all paying attention she added: "When I call out your name raise your hand and I will mark this book to show that you are here."

M. Benoit had left a list of students for her among many other useful items. He'd left her a note of welcome and an explanation as well.

Ma chère mademoiselle C——

Welcome to our school.

I spent a happy life here teaching the children of farmers and those who live in Montrésor. For three generations I was their teacher, but time catches up with everyone and now I must go. I knew nothing but good children here and I believe they left this place well prepared for their next step along the path of life.

Remember that if you respect them and give them of your best they will repay you with many blessings and some surprises too. You know these things already of course, but I hope you will not mind an old man reminding you of them.

Our school is poor in resources, but that does not prevent a good teacher, as I'm sure you are, from teaching well. Cleverness and enthusiasm can compensate for many shortcomings. In the springtime, when the countryside is green and full of new life, your charges will learn more from studying the natural world than they will from the finest textbooks. A blank sheet of paper and coloured chalks will set their imaginations free.

Although all your students are good children, some of them have small problems you should know about. The twins Mathilde and Vincent are mischievous; keep them apart in class or they will be disruptive and never learn. Antoine's father has a problem with alcohol and Gérard's father was recently killed in a tractor accident on his farm. Maryse is a slow learner, but she is not stupid and eventually understands. The rest of the children you will have no problems with.

Even Armand will not be difficult for you, although he is special in ways you will find hard to understand. This school was built in 1871 and Armand's name appeared on the roll in the very first year. You will argue as I did that Armand is a common name among boys, but as your students grow older and move on to other schools, you will find that Armand remains. He was my student for all my years in Montrésor. He sits quiet and unmoving through all his lessons, is not there when play-time comes and vanishes when school is over. The desk at the back is know as 'Armand's desk'. When I was first at this school I went close to Armand and spoke to him, but felt only a cold emptiness wash over me. I tried to take his hand but he withdrew until I moved away. I should have listened to my predecessor, as I hope you will listen to me. Leave Armand alone, he will not trouble you.

Ma chère mademoiselle C——, I hope your time at Montrésor will be as happy as was mine.

Pierre Benoit

****

"Mathilde and Vincent, I do not want you to sit next to each other. Vincent, move to that desk next to Maryse." Vincent started to protest, but when he saw that Mademoiselle C—— was serious he plodded his way to Maryse. "That is your seat every day now Vincent. You must sit nowhere else. Do you understand?"

"Yes maîtresse."

Isabelle looked at her students, their eyes bright, their faces expectant, occasional soft whispers one child to another were all that broke the silence. Only Armand, the boy-shaped darkness in his dark corner, now troubled her.

"Armand, won't you come and sit with the other children," she implored.

The older children giggled, they knew not to talk to Armand, they all turned to look towards the dark corner.

"Now children, you know that I am your new teacher, but I know nothing of you. I want you all to tell me a little about yourselves."

One by one she fired questions at each of the children. Most answered readily enough and she learned small things about them, fact and fantasy intermingled. Finally only Armand was left.

She walked to his desk, determined to persuade him to respond. He sat solid, substantial, looking not at her but through her, his face grim. His clothing was strange and old fashioned. Empty coldness washed over her.

She turned away.

"Who can tell me about Armand?" She asked the class.

One boy stood up.

"The curé says that Armand lives with Jesus and that we should be happy for him."

Isabelle looked at the boy. She didn't ask if he believed the curé. Instead she shivered.

She became accustomed to Armand's presence. For a time she asked questions of the old folk of Montrésor, those who must know something, but she received only denials. The mayor told her she was upsetting people, that she should ask no more questions. Isabelle concurred.

After her first few days as the teacher of Montrésor she stopped thinking about Armand, stopped wondering. She was a good teacher, the people of the village were glad she taught their children and she stayed there for many years.

Snake

As snow blown by the breeze drifted in beneath the cottage door he shivered. It was that time of year again. Logs harvested during the dry months of summer crackled and blazed noisily in the hearth, sparks and smoke swirled up the chimney, the logs gave off ample heat—but still he shivered.

He put his book aside, rose from his chair and crossed to the door. With his right foot he tapped the long knitted snake he used as a draught excluder back into place, just as he had done four or five times already that evening. Each time, at a point he never noticed, the snake was pushed aside again, as though the door had silently opened. This was a winter ritual he had become accustomed to, it happened only when the nights were long and dark and cold. At first it had troubled him and he sought an explanation, but when the only possible explanation left was irrational, he stopped worrying and just accepted what was.

All through the spring, summer and autumn he loved his cottage. Through the windows, from the open door, from his seat in the garden, he watched the seasons burgeon, change and die, until at last winter came. Even then he still loved the place, but it too changed. From picture perfect it changed to dark and brooding, from inviting it changed to merely accepting of his presence.

He returned to his chair, picked up his whisky glass and let the dancing flames cast light through its tawny colour. Winter was always the season of whisky for him and he'd stocked up with his favourite cold filtered single malt. Forty-eight percent proof it was, and on brooding nights like this it returned the glow of summer to his soul. Finishing what was left in his glass he poured another and then returned to his book.

****

When he'd purchased the cottage a few years earlier it had been all but derelict. It was structurally sound and, even though tiles were missing, the roof still kept the rain out were the best the agents could say for it.

Tap water came from an underground spring, there was no electricity, no gas. It was impossible to tell where the garden stopped and the surrounding woodland began. An overgrown track led to the nearest road, and from there it was two miles to the village. It was exactly what he had been looking for.

His nearest neighbour was a small estate church. Once it had served the need to worship of a wealthy family and their large staff of servants, gardeners, farm workers and gamekeepers. Now the house was a pile of rubble clothed in grass and weeds and the only people left were those buried in the churchyard that was separated from his garden by a crumbling brick wall.

After buying the cottage he did the work that was necessary to make it liveable. He fixed broken windows and had electricity installed. He cleared the track to the road enough to enable him to get his car close to the building. He had the water supply checked. Over the years since then he'd gradually improved each room until he had a home that reminded him of his parents home, a place where love could survive, where he would be comfortable.

He'd escaped from a marriage that had been loveless for years. Staying together had been a convenience, all feeling lost in a constant war over possessions, money, property—a war that was ultimately won or lost over possession of a single CD. When that point came he'd left without even saying goodbye. The next day he filed for divorce, and as acrimonious as that turned out to be, as tiring, as upsetting, when it was over he felt like a free man again.

He settled down in 'The Cottage'—it needed no other

name—and rebuilt his happiness. One day, he knew, perhaps quite soon, he would be happy enough to look for company again—perhaps even love.

Re-immersed in writing the kind of prose that was unsatisfying, but that paid the bills, he dreamed of completing the novel that he hadn't returned too since he'd been here. When he could return to that he would believe that his renaissance was complete.

****

He rose from his chair again, crossed to the door again, and with his right foot he again tapped the long knitted snake he used as a draught excluder back into place. It was far too heavy to be constantly blown aside by the breeze beneath the door, but he'd thought of fixing it to the bottom of the door anyway. He hadn't got around to it yet. Tomorrow. Maybe he would do that tomorrow. Even as the thought occurred to him he decided he wouldn't fix it tomorrow. One day he would though, definitely.

****

This had been his home for three years before he decided to go and look at the church.

Regular freelance writing work, the process of turning the cottage into a home, the pleasures of solitude and silence, had all kept him busy until one summer afternoon, quite suddenly, he thought 'I must go and look at the church.'

He downed his gardening tools and found a gap in the boundary wall where he could cross into the graveyard. He made his way between headstones and tussocks of long grass. He reached the porch of the church.

To his surprise the building appeared to be in a good state of repair and the door was solid and closed. When he opened the door it swung easily inwards, with only the slightest squeaking from dry hinges.

Rainbows of light streamed in through stained glass windows, and as his eyes adjusted they were drawn towards the natural focus of the pulpit. Even from forty feet away he could see that it had been carved by a master-craftsman. Made from heavy, dark wood, the front panel bore a carved relief of Noah and his ark. Beside the pulpit, a board with two hymn numbers, 74 and 147, hung on a stone column. It was as if the hymns would soon be sung again. He was not a religious man, but so many hymns were familiar that he wondered if he knew them.

On the altar, in front of a large, gilt crucifix, a vase of flowers that could be no more than a few days old added a touch of life to this cold and empty space. He surmised at once that an old lady from the village, probably a very old lady, still thought it was her duty to tend for this forgotten place of worship.

He stood silently for a moment or two, and then decided not to disturb the peace of the place with the clatter of his boots across the stone floor.

Back in the churchyard he breathed deeply of the fragrant summer air. It was only when he recognised the scents of grass and wild flowers that he realised that inside the church the smell had been of mildew and decay.

****

Without knowing why, he never knew why, he looked towards his door and saw that the snake had moved inwards again. The winter breeze was so slight that if there was a draught it didn't bother him, but still he rose from his chair, crossed to the door, and with his right foot he pushed the long knitted snake back into place.

Resettled in his chair he poured himself another whisky, sipped it and sighed contentedly.

****

As he crossed back through the churchyard to his garden, he stopped to look at some of the headstones. The grandest were obviously those of the family who had owned the big house. Once, they would have been ostentatious, now, despite their position of prominence, a position in which God would look favourably on them, they were as weathered and broken as the lesser stones. Montague was the family, and here were the last resting places of those who had died young and those who had lived a full life, those who had been loved and those who had been disliked.

He walked among the lesser stones reading names, wondering who these people who had lived only to serve had been. Jones. Peters. Donaldson. Montague, maybe a cousin or other family member from much lower in the pecking order of preference. Simpkins. Even a Spooner, his own family name. Edward Spooner, born 1861, died 1910. Not much missed or much loved according to the very plain name and dates on the headstone. Here Edward Spooner was though, in death the equal of his master and everyone else buried here.

****

He closed his book and put it aside. His eyes were tired. It was time to sleep. He picked up his whisky glass and sipped what was left as he watched the logs in the fireplace collapse into a mound of glowing embers. Sparks danced their way up the chimney to the night-time darkness, but there was no smoke now. He felt content.

As he sat, he felt the coldness brush against his cheek. It was like a hand, gentle, caressing. It always came on winter nights when he was enjoying the last wakeful moments of the night. He shivered. It wasn't a shiver of dread or fear or even of coldness, it was just something he would prefer not to feel.

Again the coldness brushed against him, and again and again. Each time he felt its touch he shivered. He finished his whisky. He stood up. He reached for the poker and prodded the embers for a few minutes until their glow dulled. Then he said softly, as he always did:

"Go away, go away, you are not welcome here."

It would be like this until the lighter evenings of spring.

"Go away, go away, you are not welcome here," he said again.

Then he crossed to the door and with his right foot he tapped the long knitted snake he used as a draught excluder back into place again, just as he had done so many times that evening.

The Old Joanna

Each time he passed the derelict building, Michael thought of his father; it was as if the boarded-up windows and the decaying stucco-coated walls called to him, saying 'remember, remember'.

Tonight, he paused and looked up. Once, a large, painted sign had hung from a decorative metal bracket, but that had long since been removed. He remembered that it had squeaked as it swung back and forth in the breeze—if there was one—or the wind in times of rougher weather. Sometimes, it had seemed to him, that it squeaked for no reason at all, but his father had told him, 'there's always a reason for everything', when he'd asked. Now, only the name-board, affixed to the wall above the door and windows, reminded those who needed reminding, that the building had once been a pub. Those who knew about pub names would know that it had been called The Rising Sun, enough carefully crafted letters still stood in relief to give that away, caked with twenty or more years of dust and grime, their gilt still glinted in the light of street lamps here and there.

Michael remembered that it was here that he'd first started to learn about the mysteries of adulthood, although, as it turned out, they weren't mysteries at all really, they were just the things that people did.

He must have been about nine years old when he first became aware of The Rising Sun. His father had arrived home from work, and, after washing, had changed into his smart trousers and a freshly ironed shirt. By then the evening meal was ready, and the family sat around the kitchen table chattering about the day as they ate. Nothing momentous had happened to any of them, but Michael's sister had lost a tooth, and was excited at the prospect of the tooth-fairy visiting. Those were the days when small things mattered, and Michael knew, now, that small things were the mortar that bound a family together.

"Are you off to the pub then, seeing as you're all dressed up?" His mother asked his father as dinner ended.

"I thought I would, if you don't mind that is."

"Of course I don't mind, you deserve your beer after working hard all day. I'll wash the dishes, get the kids to bed, and then relax a bit."

"I thought I might take Mikey with me, for a while, he'll have to learn about alcohol one day, and I'd rather he learned from me."

"Oh…" his mother said, "I suppose you know best dear. But don't be too late back."

****

During the summer, it had seemed to Michael, some nights were so warm and daylight lasted so long, that it didn't get dark almost until morning. His first visit to The Rising Sun had been one of those nights.

As he skipped along the street holding his father's hand, he felt almost as if he was about to become a proper grown-up.

"Will I have beer like you, daddy?" He asked.

His father laughed.

"No, you'll stay in the beer garden. There might be other children like you there, and there's a swing to play on. You're not old enough to go inside the pub yet. I'll bring you lemonade, and you can pretend it's beer."

Michael was disappointed, the shine had been taken off his first step along the road to manhood, but he was almost there, he knew he was, and his feeling of disappointment soon evaporated.

When they reached The Rising Sun, he father led him past the main entrance and through a side door marked 'Beer Garden'. There were wooden tables and benches, the promised swing, but no other children. On three sides of the warden was a high trellis fence, with unweeded beds of neglected roses against it. Two ancient ladies sat at one of the tables with their drinks.

"Hello dear, you come to get drunk with your daddy," one said, then they both laughed with toothless mouths.

Michael drew back from the women and grabbed his father's hand, but his father pushed him away.

"Don't be silly, Mikey. Go and play on the swing and I'll be back soon with your lemonade."

"Only lemonade," the same woman said, "poor, deprived little mite," and they laughed again.

Michael backed away from his father, in the direction of the swing, and only when he guessed he was at a safe distance from the women did he turn his back. By the time he was swinging back and forth, listening to the chain that held the seat squeak for lack of oil, his father had vanished. He returned a few minutes later with a glass of lemonade, and called to Michael. By then Michael had watched the two women leave, cackling to themselves, so he hurried to the table where his father had left the lemonade and slowly sipped it, while imagining how grown-up he would look to his friends—if only they could see him.

****

Over the next few years, Michael often went to The Rising Sun with his father on long summer evenings, and the older he became the later they stayed. During those visits, he learned numerous things about pubs. Mainly that he would not be permitted to enter the bar for many, many years. So he sat in the garden, sipped his lemonade, and learned. He learned what to do with the blue twist of salt that he always found in his bag of Smith's Potato Crisps—only the finest British potatoes used. He learned that there were two bars, the public bar where the men drank their beer and talked noisily about important things such as football and the young female assistant in the newsagent's shop, and the 'snug', where the ladies sat and gossiped idly, as his father once explained to him, while they drank their port and lemon or half pints of shandy. He learned later still, that the pungent aroma that escaped into the garden every time the door was opened, was from an almost necromantic blend of the odours of brown ale, urine and Black Beauty Shag.

Sometimes, unseen, to him, hands would tinkle on the joanna as he heard it called, an old, upright piano that he would one day see for himself. A sing-song would begin, all the songs, what his father called the greatest hits of World War One, were sung with great gusto, but Michael could never join in.

By the time he could enter the bar, the days of sing-songs were long over, the spittoons had been turned into plant holders, and the piano was covered with potted plants and had become no more than part of the décor.

His father lost interest in The Rising Sun once it was gentrified. He said it sold nothing but lager and gassy beer and, anyway, all the people were unreal. He said they seemed to be alive, but that's all, they just seemed to be alive. Michael hadn't fully understood, then, what his father had meant, but, as the years passed, he learned.

By the time of his eighteenth birthday, Michael's father had descended into old age, even though he was not officially old. Two years later he died. Michael wanted to believe that his father's decline was caused by modernity, he often grumbled to his son about how rapid change wasn't right, how people needed time to adapt, but he knew that his father's death was really the result of a serious illness.

That left just Michael and his mother.

Although he loved his mother, she showed no interest in him or life in general. As long as she had a bottle of gin to drink and a TV soap to watch, she was as happy as she would ever be. She didn't outlive his father by more than five years, and the family doctor told Michael, who was by then about twenty-three years old, that his mother had died of liver disease. Alcoholism was the true cause, he knew. Suicide by gin, he'd thought as he wept.

He'd tried to convince himself that his grief was real, but he questioned that, always. He'd grieved for his real mother from soon after the death of his father, as he watched her change into someone he didn't know. By the time her liver stopped working, she was a shell of the mother he'd loved, whose conversation consisted of 'I love you, Mikey' and 'buy me a bottle on your way home'. After a while, he stopped buying her gin, but, as alcoholics always do, she found other ways to obtain her favourite drink.

****

All this passed through his mind as he stood and looked at the boarded-up pub, but he felt as if he'd stepped outside himself and lived his life again at high speed.

"It's gonna be pulled down," the voice of a middle-aged man who'd paused beside him, brought Michael back to awareness. "Crying shame if you ask me, this was my dad's boozer."

"My dad's too," Michael replied, but the stranger was already walking away.

****

He looked up at the sad, sad building one last time before he shrugged his shoulders and walked away, towards his home—the house he'd inherited from his mother, knowing that tomorrow he would stop to look at the old pub again, to reminisce, to remember, to wonder.

Home was a depressing place, a place he just couldn't be bothered with. There was dust everywhere, and in the corner of the hallway a pile of his mother's old knitting magazines. He'd never seen her knit, he didn't even know if she'd known how to knit, but she had enjoyed looking at the styles. He knew he should have got rid of those magazines, but they were memories, a link to the past, to his childhood and happiness, and they had to remain. Every speck of dust was a ghost to him, a word, a mood, a moment from long ago. What would happen if he disturbed such ghosts he didn't know, so he let them be.

In the kitchen, which with his bedroom and the bathroom, were the only rooms he ever cleaned, he took a frozen dinner out and stuck it in the microwave. He set the cooking time, pushed the start button and waited. Soon the machine would ping, like a butler sounding the dinner gong in its own small way, and he would eat.

After his meal he stretched out on his bed. He'd already forgotten what he'd eaten, after all, one frozen dinner is pretty much the same as the next. He reached for his book and started to read, but, just as he always did, after a few minutes he put the book aside, and let his thoughts wander to the shadows cast by the light into the corners of his room. Those shadows were a constant, unless a draught moved the ceiling light they were always the same. He wondered, as he always did, what hid in them; things he didn't know about, maybe even things he could never imagine.

****

"Smugglers," his father said to him, one sunny evening in the beer garden of The Rising Sun, "did you know smugglers used this pub. There's a big cellar down below, and they filled it with their contraband. Imagine that, real smugglers, Mikey." He deposited a glass of lemonade and a bag of crisps in front of Michael. "Be a good boy." Then he went back into the bar.

Shortly after that, someone started to play the piano, and the words of songs he didn't know drifted to his ears.

Michael did know about the smugglers, but no more than his father had just told him, for he said the same words at least once every visit, never more, never less. Michael had once begged his father to tell him more about the smugglers, but it became clear over the years that he'd already told all that he knew.

****

A few weeks later, Michael was surprised to see that the boarded-up windows of The Rising Sun had been uncovered, the front entrance was open, and the empty pub echoed with the sounds of banging, loud male voices and laughter.

He stopped, as he always did, and looked. He couldn't remember when he'd last seen those windows, shattered and dust covered though they now were, but it had certainly been many years before. He peered through one of the windows, into the public bar. Inside, it was gloomier than he'd expected it to be, and as his eyes adjusted to the poor light, he saw that the large room was broken and sad and dead. Nothing indicated that it had once held all the life he remembered. The bar was still there, but the once-trendy wine-bar fittings and furnishings had all been removed. Like the bar, his memories were still there too, he knew they were, and in the corner where it had always sat, was the old piano. Unloved for years, but too heavy to move, it had been left to decay like the building itself.

****

When he thought about it later, he couldn't pin down what had made him walk into the old bar room and call out. He'd heard someone shout out 'see who that is, Jack', as he went to the piano. He lifted the lid and depressed a few keys, they still worked, but the sound that came from the piano was as tired and dusty as the room itself.

"What you doin' in 'ere," a man, Jack maybe, had said from behind him. "You ain't got no right bein' in 'ere you know."

"What's happening?" He'd asked.

"Old place is bein' pulled down, good job too, it's been an eyesore for too long."

"Remembering. My father used to drink here—me too when I was old enough. People used to sing around this piano."

"That's nice," the man said, "but you ain't got no right bein' in 'ere. You should go."

"What's going to happen to the piano?" He'd asked.

"No one wants those old things now, it will be carted away to the dump. Now go."

"I want it."

"You want it, you must be crazy," the man laughed as he spoke. "Take it with you now, will you?"

"I want it," Michael had reiterated, "really I do."

"Alright, I'll ask," the man had said reluctantly. "Got an idiot here who wants that old pianer," Michael heard the man shout out a few seconds later.

"Let him have it, Jack, twenty and it's his."

****

Michael found a removal company who agreed to collect the piano from The Rising Sun and deliver it to his home a few days later—for an exorbitant price.

126

He'd been spurred into doing some housework while he waited.

His mother's knitting magazines went to the recycling bin, her empty gin bottles too; the hallway was free of dust, free of words and memories. In the 'parlour', as his mother always called it, he'd dusted and tidied and cleared out old things that he really didn't need any more, he'd known he hadn't needed them for years, but like the dust they were a link to his past, like physical memories.

Then the piano arrived.

Four men had difficulty manipulating it into the house, but finally, in all its dusty magnificence, it was in the corner he'd cleared for it.

He found a piano tuner, a blind man, because someone had told him that blind people made the best piano tuners.

Before the man arrived three days later he cleaned and dusted and polished that old piano—right down to the wires—much more than he'd ever cleaned anything before.

There were circular marks from beer glasses on its lid, he didn't even think of trying to remove them. He fingered them, traced their shape with a forefinger, and wanted, so very much wanted, one of them to be from a beer glass placed by his father.

Once the piano was tuned, he got pleasure from striking its keys, he couldn't play, but he was determined that he would learn. Sometimes he thought that the key sequences he struck sounded like the music of Stravinsky.

****

On days when he wasn't working, Michael took to visiting the chic coffee shop opposite The Rising Sun. It offered all kinds of exotic-sounding beverages, but all he ever wanted was strong, black coffee.

From its window, he watched the demolition of the pub progress. The chimneys were removed, the slate roof-tiles were removed and stacked, and brick by brick the nineteenth century building slowly vanished.

He watched dust as it rose into the air, as it swirled in the breeze. In it he saw the faces of those patrons he'd come to know years ago. He saw his father's face too, and he was smiling.

The clatter of the demolition became piano music, the memory of the old joanna, as the ghosts of yesterday sang the greatest hits of World War One for the final time.

Fog-Tree

Every time Alistair came close to the big house he heard the rattle of bones. Today was no different.

He smiled ruefully to himself and crossed the road to avoid walking near the overgrown gates and the dark, heavy trees that surrounded them. There was no awful sound coming from that house. His fear was irrational. He knew it was irrational, but steering clear of the place was something he'd done since childhood, when walking past those gates had brought terror to his heart.

****

Each year when his grandfather visited he would walk the nearby country lanes with the old man, clutching the bony hand and asking all the 'why' questions his young mind could conceive.

"Why don't the clouds fall out of the sky grandpa?"

"Why do people get old grandpa?"

"Why is rain wet grandpa?

"Why is your hand so bony grandpa?"

Usually the old man would chuckle, tousle his grandson's hair and answer "just because".

It was years later, after his grandfather's death that Alistair realized he answered 'just because' just because he didn't know the answers.

They regularly passed the gates of the big house on those walks and neither of them were bothered by the branches that groaned and the leaves that rustled, even on the stillest, warmest of summer days.

Over the course of several summers his grandpa changed. It was his parents who noticed first.

"There's something wrong with dad," Alistair heard his father whisper to his mother.

"What do you mean?"

"He's forgetting things. He gets frustrated when he can't manage to do simple tasks and he loses his temper easily."

"He's growing old dear, he's just growing old, it's natural," his mother said, her gentle voice soothing.

Alistair changed too. As he grew older he became more curious and asked more questions. He demanded proper answers of his grandpa as they went on their rural perambulations. Sometimes grandpa tried to explain, but his confusion was apparent even to an eight year old. Over the course of just a few days the old man became so absent minded that he forgot the route home, and it was left to Alistair to guide him. He still clutched the tough, bony hand just as he had when he was five, and even at so young an age Alistair noticed the tremor the old man could no longer hide.

When he was at family home, the old man sat in the chair his mother called 'grandpa's chair'. In earlier years he would hold animated conversations with anyone who would listen; he would thumb through the newspaper, his eyes lingering, widening when he reached the page that Alistair was never allowed to see.

"What is it grandpa, what is it?" Alistair would scuttle forward and try to peer at the forbidden page, but grandpa always held it close to his chest.

"It's something only grown-up people should see. It's not for little boys like you."

Alistair would sulk, but soon forget.

Now grandpa sat in his chair staring vacantly, his eyes unfocused, his hands on his legs.

"I think it might be dementia," his mother said one Sunday afternoon.

"No. It can't be, it can't be." His father sounded angry.

"I'll take him to the doctor tomorrow."

"If it is dementia, what will we do? He goes home next weekend, he won't be able to cope."

Alistair's mother saw him listening to the conversation.

"Take your grandpa for a walk, Alistair," she said.

****

As they walked the lanes in the mellow, late summer warmth Alistair held grandpa's hand as his mother had instructed him to do. They dawdled past hedgerows laden with blackberries ripe for picking, breathed in the scent of freshly mown hay.

Alistair asked a question or two, but grandpa didn't answer; he just shuffled along beside his grandson, the roles of child and chaperone reversed in all but age.

Occasionally grandpa would start to speak, but his words tailed off unfinished. He would stop abruptly and point at the sky or a tree or a stone on the road, but could never explain the reason for his interest.

He started to sing a song he'd sung with Alistair many times and Alistair joined in. For a while it was the way it had always been between grandpa and grandson.

Frère Jacques, frère Jacques
Dormez-vous, dormez-vous?
Sonnez les matines, sonnez les matines
Ding-dang-dong, ding-dang-dong

After that he managed to speak coherently as they walked, and Alistair was happy that grandpa was back.

The music of bell ringers practicing in the parish church echoed across the countryside, sounding tuneless to Alistair's ear. Bees flitted from flower to flower, birds swooped about doing what birds do when they are not building nests.

He and grandpa stopped at a gated field to watch cows grazing.

"No rain today," grandpa said as he stared at the cloudless afternoon sky. "When it's going to rain, cows sit down you know."

They both fell silent as little by little they completed their circuitous walk. Soon they would be home for tea, and the cake mother had baked.

"Why do these trees always groan grandpa?" Alistair asked when they reached the big house. He felt grandpa's hand tighten on his until it hurt.

"Questions, questions," grandpa yelled, "I'll teach you not to ask questions."

He jerked on Alistair's arm and dragged him towards the gates of the big house. Alistair went along, alarmed by the sudden change in grandpa.

Inside the gates he saw the large, boarded-up building with slates missing from it's roof. He could see that it had been white painted once. The garden was an overgrown jungle of brambles, weeds and plants gone wild. Improbably, a sundial poked out from a patch of brambles. All around trees like those by the gates sighed and groaned for no discernible reason. Grandpa stopped and pointed.

"That tree, that one over there... you see it don't you... that's the Fog Tree. See how there's a mist all through its branches. I was scared of this place when I was a boy like you, because in that mist is a creature that eats boys who ask too many questions." Grandpa chuckled and started to drag Alistair towards the mist shrouded tree.

"No, grandpa, no," Alistair shouted. He dug his heels into the moss covered ground and pulled back as hard as he could. Tears were streaming from his eyes. "No, grandpa, no."

"Tears won't do you any good if you get near the Fog Tree, boy. Stop asking so many questions. Now let's go home."

****

Next day grandpa disappeared.

"He must have wandered off," Alistair's mother said.

Both his parents were frantic with worry, his mother cried a lot, his father was morose.

Alistair didn't worry at all. He decided he'd stopped loving his grandpa. He played with his toys, he played with his friends. He sung the song he'd sung with grandpa over and over until his mother told him to stop:

Frère Jacques, frère Jacques
Dormez-vous, dormez-vous?
Sonnez les matines, sonnez les matines
Ding-dang-dong, ding-dang-dong

****

He crossed back over the road once he'd passed the big house, he really would have to try and break the habit.

He remembered that the police search for grandpa had gone on for weeks before it was quietly dropped. They'd searched everywhere, even the big house and its grounds. Eventually his parents stopped mentioning grandpa. He'd been declared dead. His estate had been settled. He was a memory.

Alistair forgot all about the old man. Although sometimes, in his dreams he heard

Frère Jacques, frère Jacques
Dormez-vous, dormez-vous?
Sonnez les matines, sonnez les matines
Ding-dang-dong, ding-dang-dong

It wasn't until he was seventeen years old that thoughts of grandpa troubled him again.

****

It was dark. He'd slept. He'd dreamed and his dreams had turned into a nightmare.

He was in the garden of the big house and he could find no way out. The gates were so overgrown that he could not even find them. All around him, the tall trees, heavy with leaves, groaned and sighed, their branches creaking as they tried to reach down to him. Across the tangle of brambles and plants a pathway opened up. It led straight to the Fog Tree. Taller, darker more threatening even than the other trees, the Fog Tree beckoned him. It called his name over and over.

Alistair. Alistair. Alistair.

There was no threat in the voice. It was kind. It was reasonable. It was grandpa's voice.

Alistair. Alistair. Alistair.

Come sing with me Alistair, come sing with me.

Alistair. Alistair. Alistair.

He found himself walking the pathway towards the Fog Tree, and watching, terrified, as he heard the swirling mist in its branches singing

Frère Jacques, frère Jacques
Dormez-vous, dormez-vous?
Sonnez les matines, sonnez les matines
Ding-dang-dong, ding-dang-dong

****

"I know where grandpa is," Alistair said over breakfast the next morning.

His parents, who'd been talking about the latest TV talent show fell silent and stared at him.

"You what?" They said in unison.

"I know where grandpa is."

He was showered with questions, and, after he had explained, he was showered with denials.

"That talk of the Fog Tree is just silliness to frighten naughty children, don't talk about it. I grew up with that story."

There was anger in his father's voice, but more discussion followed and gradually his parents calmed down enough to listen.

"Come with me and I'll show you," Alistair said when he'd told them of both his visit to the big house with grandpa and his nightmare again.

****

They pushed open the gates of the big house together. The wooden slats were rotten, the hinges were rusted, only a thick growth of trailing weeds held them up.

"Go over and look," Alistair challenged.

His father moved forward a few paces and stopped.

"I'm not going over there," he said.

Around them the trees made their familiar sighing and groaning sounds.

134

"Listen." Alistair had moved forward to stand beside his father.

They both heard a sound like that of a wooden xylophone coming from the misty canopy of the Fog Tree.

"What the..." his father started.

"The rattle of bones," Alistair said.

In his mind he saw an image of ribs and tibias and clavicles and scapulas hanging unclear in the Fog Tree's branches. They danced against one another and made music. He began to sing, softly, oh so softly

Frère Jacques, frère Jacques
Dormez-vous, dormez-vous?
Sonnez les matines, sonnez les matines
Ding-dang-dong, ding-dang-dong

The Violinist

Each morning he awoke as the church clock chimed seven. It had been that way for years—never six, never eight, always seven—winter or summer, it made no difference.

Ding, ding, ding, ding, ding, his eyes would open, *ding, ding,* and he was fully awake. He had puzzled for many years over why this should be; the *dinging* of the clock was almost genteel, not at all like the bombastic, booming church clock in his neighbourhood when he was a boy.

He left his bed immediately. He showered. He shaved. He dressed carefully in a well pressed suit, a clean white shirt, a tie. With brightly shining, black, lace-up shoes on his feet, he went through to the kitchen. He prepared a breakfast of fresh fruit and Earl Grey tea. He ate slowly. He sipped slowly. Throughout his eighty years he had been an unhurried man. He saw no reason to change his habits now.

When breakfast was over, he collected his violin case from near the door of his apartment. Covered with real leather, it was battered and worn, but he would never change it. His father had given it to him when he was a young man, almost fifty-five years ago. He placed the case upon the kitchen table, opened it and gently lifted out his violin. He had never wanted to own a Stradivarius, although he admired them greatly; instead his chosen instrument had been made by Anton Fischer in Vienna in the mid-19th century. To him, it was the finest violin that had ever been made and it had lasted him a lifetime.

Every morning, before going out, he polished the veneer of the instrument, he plucked the strings, retuned when necessary, applied rosin to the hairs of his bow, and played a short piece to ensure that all was well. Then he placed the violin and the bow back in their case, adjusted his tie in the hallway mirror and, carrying his violin in its case, left his home.

He was in the habit of purchasing a carnation, or other seasonal flower, for his buttonhole from an old lady who sold flowers by the entrance to the metro station. As she saw him approach, she smiled.

"Just the thing for you this morning, dearie," she said cheerily as she handed him a pink carnation, "as fresh as a daisy that one is."

He smelled the flower as he slipped some coins into the woman's hand, it didn't matter how much the carnation cost, a transaction such as this had taken place almost every day since they were both young. The scent of the flower was as fragrant as the summer morning itself.

"Thank you," he said. Then he smiled at her and crossed the road as he headed towards the park gates.

When he reached the delicatessen, he entered and ordered a sandwich; the time was just approaching nine o'clock and there were no other customers.

"The usual, sir?" The owner asked.

"The usual," he agreed, "thank you." 'The usual' meant thick slices of corned beef with sliced tomato and French mustard, in well buttered, seeded, malt bread. As with the purchase of the carnation for his buttonhole, this too was a daily ritual—even on Sundays. "Also a bottle of Perrier water to take with me please."

He reached into his pocket, and pulled out coins to pay the man; the owner handed him the water. They both smiled. They thanked each other again. They were both punctilious in their politeness.

There had been a time, he recalled, when they had used each other's names, formally of course, as Mr ———— and Mr ————, but they had stopped using them, and now, he was sure, they were forgotten.

"The boy will bring your lunch at the usual time, sir, you can be sure of that," the owner said by way of concluding their transaction.

He nodded in gratitude. He smiled. He left the delicatessen shop and continued on his way.

When he reached the news vendor just outside the park gates, he stopped and purchased his usual daily. He folded the newspaper and tucked it under his arm, he would read it in the evening when he returned to his apartment. He deposited payment on the cover of a garish-looking magazine; the news vendor grunted. This too happened every morning, the man always grunted, but they had an understanding of sorts.

He was glad to enter the park, for the street he left was busy with people now, and noisy with traffic. Somehow, the iron gates of the park, wide open though they were, left in their place a barrier that instantly reduced the noise coming from the hurrying city. A few metres inside the gate, and he soon forgot the busyness outside.

Each day, as he made his way to his usual bench beneath the sheltering branches of a tree, he marvelled at the beauty around him. For all the advances in science and technology, for all that those who owned television sets claimed to be able to experience from their homes, being surrounded by such beauty was, for him, incomparable. Flowers were in full summer bloom, the leaves of trees rustled delicately, birds flew and settled and flew again, and the sun cast crisp, sharp shadows.

Apart from himself, there were other regulars in the park, those who came every day. One or two of them he had come to know a little over the years. Ahead of him, on a bench very much like his own bench, beneath a tree very much like his own tree, was Mr I-Only-Play-to-Draw. Like the delicatessen, he'd known the man's name once, but the name had ceased to matter when he accepted that only what the man did had any importance.

"Good morning," he said when he reached Mr I-Only-Play-to-Draw, "what a very fine day it is."

Mr I-Only-Play-to-Draw did not reply immediately, his right hand hovered for a moment over the chess board he'd set before him on a folding card-table. Then he advanced a black pawn two squares. He was playing against himself as he always did, and he refused any offer from a stranger to play against him.

"It is indeed a very fine morning, Violin," Mr I-Only-Play-to-Draw replied. Then he returned to his game.

He smiled and walked slowly on. He'd once asked Mr I-Only-Play-to-Draw why he only played to draw.

"Because to do otherwise would be cheating," the man had replied, "for whichever colour I play as, black or white, I know what move I will make when I move for the other colour."

That had struck him as absurd, but he respected the right of Mr I-Only-Play-to-Draw to believe whatever he wished.

He passed by The Scribbler, the woman who spent her time writing in a large notebook, they had never exchanged a word, or even a smile, so intent was she on what she was doing. He passed too, the man who had no designation, because he had no idea what he was doing, and The Man Who Cries, whose sadness seemed so ineffable that to even think of engaging him in conversation would be to intrude.

By and by, he came close to He-Who-Talks-Bird. This man interested him greatly. They had never spoken, but they always nodded and smiled in that polite way of strangers. He could hear He-Who-Talks-Bird when he was still a good few metres from him, for the man sat on his bench, and with his lips pursed he made bird-like whistling sounds. For their part, it was as if the birds understood, for they clustered on the ground around the man's feet, settled on the bench beside him, and even rested on his shoulders. Whenever the man paused for a moment, the birds would talk back to him, first one, then two, then three, until there was a cacophony of birdsong. Then the man would smile and begin his whistling again. It was a rare gift to have.

He walked on. He passed a bed of fragrant roses where the bees were busily harvesting. He walked on. He passed the fountain, already seeming languid in the early morning heat; it burbled gently as it sent flashing droplets all around. Later, a child or two would be brought here to play, but even they would recognise that the park was a place of peace, their laughter would be muted, their chatter would be quiet, because that's the way they always were.

Finally, he reached his bench, beneath his tree and sat.

He removed his violin from its case, his bow too, and set them on the bench beside him. He placed his newspaper in the empty case, and closed it. Then he placed the case beneath the bench on which he sat. He took a folded, white handkerchief from the pocket of his jacket, and used it to remove any trace of perspiration that might be on his hands. He picked up his violin, caressed it gently, just as one might caress the face of a loved one. He lifted it to his shoulder, and, with the chinrest beneath his chin, he began to play.

He liked to play the music he had learned as a young man, when he had been a violinist with a great orchestra. That was long ago, before the war had put an end to his dream of being famous among his own people. Persecuted, he'd crossed his ruptured, broken country until he managed to reach the frontier of a peaceful nation, and from there he had come to this welcoming land with nothing but the clothes he was wearing and the violin his father had given him. He named his violin 'Peace', for peace was all he wanted, but he had never told anyone that.

Over many years he played with a number of orchestras, he became a renowned soloist, he was admired, but he always felt like a stranger here in this country that had welcomed him. Like the names of the flower-seller, the delicatessen owner and Mr I-Only-Play-to-Draw, there came a time when his own name was no longer important. He was retired. He had no need of a name.

He spent his days in this park, playing peaceful music on his beloved Peace, mostly for himself but also for anyone who cared to listen.

Before him now, a woman had stopped. She was neither beautiful nor ugly, she was neither young nor old. He had seen her many times. Their relationship, for as such he liked to think of it, had reached the stage where they would smile and nod at each other. So they smiled and they nodded and he played and she listened, and the music he made reached out and embraced her. As the music progressed he saw her eyes fill with tears, he saw her take a handkerchief from a pocket and dab the tears away. When he finished playing, she mouthed a 'thank you'; she knew better than to offer him money. She smiled and she walked away.

That's how his day would be. That's how his days always were. He would stop to eat when the boy brought his sandwich, he ceased playing briefly now and then to take small sips of water, otherwise he played and played the music he loved.

People came, people went, men and women, young and old. Those who came looking weary, walked away refreshed, those who came looking troubled, walked away smiling. Tears were shed, tears were dried, smiles grew, he was happy. For a while, at least, everyone who listened was healed by the peaceful music of Peace.

When five o'clock came, when people were heading home, when the park would soon be closed for the night, he stowed his violin back in its case and headed home. Every day he wondered if to come to this place and play his music was what he had always been meant to do, if all his achievements that had led him here were only stations along the way. He knew he would return tomorrow, and when he headed home tomorrow he knew he would wonder all over again.

As he neared the park gates, he saw that Mr I–Only–Play-to-Draw was putting his chess set in its box.

"Another day," he said.

"Another day," Mr I–Only–Play-to-Draw replied.

Then they nodded at each other, and they smiled at each other, and he patted his violin case then passed through the park gates and continued walking home.

Going Home

In the three years since his family home had passed to him, he hadn't visited the house at all, because he knew that painful memories were locked behind that hardwood door.

His childhood would still be packed in boxes in the attic. His father's moth-balled suits would still be hanging in the wardrobe in the largest bedroom, while his mother's clothes, skirts, blouses and pretty floral dresses, would be in the bedroom she'd taken as her own when she'd decided the time for separate rooms had arrived. He'd still been a child when that happened, barely fourteen years old as he recalled.

Downstairs, framed photographs of people would be smiling from the walls and shelves: his parents when they were young and happy, his only aunt and uncle, his grandmother. His face would be there also, as a child, a teenager and a very young man; and like the others, he would be smiling too. But not long after he'd left home, he realised that all his smiles were make believe. He'd smiled only because he'd been told to smile.

He put the key into the lock, pushed the door open, and let the smell of home come to greet him, or, at least, the smell of the house on the day of his mother's funeral. It was the smell of old-age, illness and death, the smell of gloss paint that had lingered for years, the smell of dust and newspapers and incontinence and lavatory blocks, and around all the other smells, the taint of camphor from the mothballs his father had insisted on using.

As he stepped into the hallway, a chill settled onto him; it wasn't the cold, not on a warm, early summer day, but the deep melancholy he felt that caused him to shiver. His childhood had not been a happy one, and already, although he had only just arrived, he imagined that he could hear his own sobbing coming from upstairs.

He ran a finger along the edge of a photo-frame, and disturbed a thick layer of dust. He wondered where so much dust had come from in an unoccupied house, especially as experts said that most domestic dust was tiny fragments of dried human skin. Perhaps, he thought, it was all the dust of the past finally settling for good.

Walking through to the kitchen, he turned a tap at the sink. No water came out, of course, because the supply, like those for gas and electricity, had been turned off years ago. He didn't know what caused him to do that, and even as he turned the tap to the off position again, he could hear his father yelling 'ask, ask, ask' at him, just as he had when he was a child.

Through the kitchen window, he could see that the back garden had become a jungle. For years that patch of land, all eighty feet of its length, had been his father's domain, and it was the only place where his father had ever taken an interest in showing him plants and seedlings and what they gave and what they became. His father had grown fruit and vegetables, and his mother had turned them into meals that he remembered to this day. Now, even the garden path was a jumble of self-willed vegetation, that was burgeoning after the spring rains.

Impulsively, he unlocked the kitchen door and stepped outside. There, the air was fragrant with the scent of natural life. He stood for a moment, and breathed the air and, like the stale old-lady air inside the house, it was the smell of home.

"Peter?" A frail voice queried from his right, "Is that you?"

He looked towards the fence that separated the garden from that of the house next door, and saw Mr Hampton, his friend Jonny's father, looking at him. The old man looked nothing like he remembered, but he knew it was him.

"Hello, Mr Hampton," he said, "it's me alright."

"That garden's in such a state," Mr Hampton said, "your old dad must be turning in his grave."

Peter nodded noncommittally.

"How's Jonny doing?" He said, after the usual exchange of neighbourly pleasantries, about health and growing old and the weather.

"He's fine, I think. I don't see much of him, says he doesn't like being around old age. I told him it's natural, and that he'd be old like me one day. He's still in the town. Not married yet, mind you, that really upset my dear wife, God rest her soul; she really wanted grandchildren before she died. She said grandchildren were continuity. Jonathan calls me every week, so I know he hasn't forgotten me."

"Have you got Jonny's number, maybe I'll give him a call before I leave town again?"

Mr Hampton recited a number as Peter tapped it into his phone.

"Have they built on the field yet?"

"Noooooo," Mr Hampton dragged out the word, a way of speaking that Peter remembered well, "and they never will, nowhere to put a road into it you see, leastways not without demolishing houses. It's as wild as your garden."

"I'll go and look, Mr Hampton. Excuse me."

"You do that sonny-boy, you and Jonny spent so much time there. Don't get lost in the jungle." As he walked away, he heard Mr Hampton chuckling to himself.

He took care as he made his way to the bottom of the garden, he couldn't see the path, but his feet remembered every inch of its route, and could feel the hard paving slabs his father had 'borrowed' from where he worked.

When he reached the boundary hedge, he was surprised to see that the cluster of bushes in the field beyond was still there, standing twelve feet high, or more. They were as tall as he remembered them.

He and Jonny had one day noticed a pool of bright sunshine at the heart of those bushes, and on hands and knees they'd pushed their way through to that sunshine, a patch of ground that was bare except for grass and dandelions. That small clearing became their 'camp', a private place where the world of demanding parents had seemed so far away. They'd been about nine years old.

Peter looked down, and saw that the battered struts of wood he and Jonny had used as a door through the hedge and into their other world were still in place. They'd imagined the wood was from the wreck of an ancient ship, a trireme—although they had little idea of what a trireme was—from a time when the field was an ocean and dinosaurs roamed the earth. Historical accuracy meant nothing to them, it was unimportant, and pirates in their sailing ships had happily coexisted with astronauts and Roman invaders with engine drivers.

He bent forward, slid the struts aside, disentangling them from the sprouting hedge, and looked at the opening through which they'd wriggled their way into the field—it looked impossibly small.

Impulsively, Peter took his jacket off, dropped it onto the ground, then stretched out on his stomach and began to force his shoulders through the opening. The hedge protested, but gradually let him pass, and only when his head was peering into the field, did he ask himself what he was doing. He continued anyway, and with a few snags on the way, a ripping sound from his back somewhere, grazes to his arms and grass and soil stains on his t-shirt and jeans, he was soon standing in the field looking around.

He felt as if he were nine years old again; his heart was thumping and he sensed an excitement that belonged to another time. Campions and daisies sprouted from the grass, buttercups shone like miniature suns, birds sang brightly, languid butterflies danced their colours through the air, and overhead a small aircraft droned like a giant bumblebee. It was summer, it was always summer in this field. He heard a child's voice, his voice, shout 'Jonny, Jonny' over and over. 'I'm here', Jonny called back, 'in the camp,' As Peter made his way towards the bushes, they grew taller and taller, and suddenly he was a little boy again, as small as he had been all those years ago.

****

"Password?" Jonny called out. "You can't come in without the password, you know that. If you try to come in, the dragon-guard will gobble you all up."

"Bungleworm," Peter yelled in irritation, "you know I know it's bungleworm."

"Rules are rules. Dragon-guard stand aside, and let Mr Peter into the camp."

Then Peter was on his hands and knees, crawling through the entrance to their camp, reaching behind him to pull concealing branches back into place as he went.

"What you doing?" He demanded when he was sitting opposite Jonny. It was obvious what Jonny was doing, but he asked anyway.

Their treasure chest, an old biscuit tin, was open, and all its treasures were spread out on the grass. Peter's favourite was the lead soldier his father had given to him, but Jonny, he knew, liked the battered Matchbox car best; it was small enough for even a nine year old to almost hide in a fist.

They sat and played for what seemed like ages. They drew a map showing the way to a lost city, and decided that when they were old enough they would go exploring together. They made up stories about other planets and the people who lived on them. They feasted on fruit flavoured Polos, exotic food sent to them by the ancient gods. Then they heard Bobby Locke shouting out their names.

"I know you're here, you're always here. I'll find you." Bobby was the local bully, he was two years older than Peter and much bigger, his menacing voice was never far away. But Bobby didn't know about their camp, so they fell silent, and after five minutes of bellowing, Bobby yelled, "I'll get you," as he stomped away. They remained silent for another five minutes, to be sure that Bobby had gone, and then began to talk again.

Peter felt warm pee in his underwear, as he always did when Bobby was around, but he hadn't really pissed himself in fear, not really, he told himself, as he stretched his t-shirt down to cover his groin area in case Jonny noticed.

"I peed a bit too, don't worry," Jonny said in a consoling voice, "it will soon dry."

"It's just a bit. When I was little it used to be a lot, I couldn't help it." Peter said, feeling embarrassed despite Jonny's words.

"I'll kill Bobby when I'm grown up," Jonny said.

"I'll help you," Peter offered.

Then they sat and talked about ways to kill Bobby; an arrow from Jonny's red Indian set, a bullet from Peter's toy six-shooter, a poisoned gobstopper, and half a dozen other ways to kill that seemed acceptable to them. They laughed, they smiled, they knew it was part of the game they played. They hated Bobby Locke, as much as small boys could ever hate anything or anyone—which equated to vehemently.

When they were satisfied that Bobby would be dead soon enough, and in the nastiest possible way, they returned to their game.

"If I really found a lost city, I would let you be king with me—and what fun we'd have. Music would be magic, and just by singing the right song we could have anything we wanted to eat, and gold and diamonds big as eggs, and ride a unicorn." Jonny's voice was yearning, whimsical.

"And people from Mars would come to see us, flying on giant birds with silver feathers and rubies for eyes, and bringing sweets no one ever tasted before, and the sun would always shine… the sun would always shine, even at night."

"Silly, if the sun was shining it wouldn't be night."

Peter thought about that, and knew Jonny was right. But the sun was shining now, and Bobby Locke hadn't found them, and his jeans were drying, and he was happy.

"Jonny, Jonny," a voice called out. I was Jonny's mother. "Time to go, dear."

"Where you going?" Peter asked.

"To the pictures again. My mum wants to see that film again, and I she says I have to go with her."

"What film's that then?" Peter asked, although he thought he knew.

"The Sound of Blue Sick," Jonny replied, then they both laughed as if that was the funniest thing they had ever heard—which perhaps it was.

As Peter watched, Jonny wriggled his way dutifully back through the bushes and into the field.

"'Bye," he yelled as he trotted through the coarse grass towards his home, "'bye Peter, see you tomorrow," then a few seconds later, "hide the treasure away."

When Peter looked, he was surprised to see that their treasure was nowhere to be seen. He was sitting in a clearing which had once seemed so big, but that now seemed small. He had no recollection of crawling into the opening in the centre of the stand of bushes, but here he was. His jeans were grass and soil stained but dry. He was a man, and had somehow crossed the years from childhood to now, or was it from now to childhood, as if time was a length of elastic that could be stretched at will. He had no idea why still nothing much grew in this opening, but he was glad it still existed, like a lucite block preserving mostly happy childhood memories.

****

More than twenty-five years had passed since he'd last been in this place. He'd been perhaps twelve years old when he and Jonny decided to talk about girls instead of lost cities, to worry about school exams rather than Bobby Locke—although Bobby continued to plague their lives well into their teenage years. They had abandoned their camp, forgotten their treasure, but had remained friends—friends forever, as they had once agreed.

He squirmed around to where they'd routinely hidden their biscuit tin treasure chest, a point where the bushes were thicker, and pulling the grass and thin branches aside, he was glad to see the tin was still there, still guarding their childhood secrets, concealing their childhood passions. He'd sometimes wondered if Jonny had ever returned here and reclaimed the tin, but mostly, he suspected, neither of them had thought about it. The image on the lid of that tin was burned into his memory, sleighs in the snow, beautiful women, their hands kept warm by ermine muffs, laughing, ruddy-faced children, a large house with glowing windows waiting to welcome them in—a romantic Victorian Christmas scene, from a world that never was.

Now, he could see, that image was almost gone, rusted away and existing only in his memory.

As he tugged the tin out from beneath the bushes, flakes of rust fell from it; it felt thin, it seemed to sigh and say 'my life is almost done, but you remembered me'. The lid was almost rusted in place, but, using a coin from his pocket, he scored around the join and managed to open the tin.

Inside were memories, nothing but memories, what else could they be. A lead soldier, a Matchbox car, several glass marbles, a browned and folded map of a lost city, some wax crayons, a pencil stub, a small notebook with a red paper cover, a half-eaten pack of fruit Polos. Such treasures, such memories.

Peter picked up the red notebook and flicked it open. There were messages in their secret code, a mix of symbols and letters that were meaningless to him now, a list of Martian names, all beginning with X or Y or Z, ideas for adventurous journeys they would take when they were older, and there were several games of Hangman. They'd enjoyed watching Bobby Locke die letter by letter, limb by limb for a while, and each game was headlined 'the end of Bobby Locke'.

When a single drop of water fell onto the notebook, Peter though it was rain, but the sun was still shining. When another drop fell, he wiped his eyes with the hem of his t-shirt. Memories. Memories. He'd had enough of memories—for now. He decided to leave. He placed the lid back onto the biscuit tin, and pushed it ahead of him as he wriggled his adult form back through the bushes, back through a space meant only for small boys. In the field, he stood up and headed back towards the garden of his home, carrying the tin as carefully as if it was delicate bone china.

"Pissing Pete," a voice yelled at him, "pissing Pete."

He heard a dog barking viciously, he felt his bladder grow heavy, but he didn't pee himself any more, not even for Bobby Locke. He turned around, and saw Bobby trundling towards him, now a giant of a man, with a huge belly flopping over the waistband of his trousers.

"It's you, it's really you." Bobby said.

His small, pugnacious dog, snarling and dripping saliva from its mouth, ran at Peter. Peter shoved the dog away with a foot, and snarls turned to whimpers.

"You kicked my dog! I'll get you for that." Bobby yelled. He tried to run towards Peter, but his feet and stomach conspired and dragged him to the ground. Obviously badly winded, Bobby just lay there. "I'll fucking well get you, I'll fucking well get you," he shouted over and over.

Peter made his way back into the garden of his home. Over the overgrown hedge he saw that Bobby was back on his feet.

"I'll fucking well get you for this," he yelled again.

"Bye, Bobby," Peter called back.

His feet took him back along the garden path to the house, he thought about the plans he and Jonny had made for the demise of Bobby Locke, about the games of Hangman, and he smiled. Like all bullies, Bobby Locke was seething with rage and self-loathing. He would take care of his own death, and probably quite soon, of that much Peter was now sure.

Nearing the house, he waved to Mr Hampton, who was peering from his kitchen window, 'watching the garden grow', as Jonny used to say. Mr Hampton smiled and waved back.

Inside the house, Peter decided that he was now in no mood to do what he had come here to do. As he slid the rusted biscuit tin into a supermarket carrier bag he'd taken from beneath the kitchen sink, where his parents always kept them for reuse, he knew he hadn't wasted his day coming home. Memories, he thought, memories. He'd found something that was inconsequential, of no meaning to an adult man, and yet it was real treasure, just as, all those years ago, he and Jonny had declared it to be.

He went back through the hallway, smiling at the smiling photographs that hung on the walls, back through the front door, which he locked behind him, back to his car. He put the biscuit tin carefully into the boot, he slung his jacket onto the passenger seat, then took out his phone and called Jonny Hampton.

****

"How many years has it been, Peter?" Jonny asked.

They were standing at the bar, waiting for bar staff, who were too busy talking amongst themselves to notice them.

"Are any of you actually here to serve customers?" Peter asked loudly, and to the amusement of several other customers who were also being ignored. The two young men and one young woman glared at him in exactly the same way, as if disdain was something they had learned to master on a company training course.

"What do you want?" The woman asked as she ambled forward. The two men disappeared into the still-room, ignoring the other waiting customers.

"Seven years, eight years at least," Peter said as he turned his head towards Jonny and answered his question.

"I asked what you want," the woman said, obviously annoyed.

"Oh, I'm sorry," Peter smiled at her, "I thought to be ignored was what was expected here."

"You trying to be funny or something?"

"Not at all."

"That's the trouble with old blokes like you, no patience. What do you want?"

Old blokes like you, that stung Peter, as he wasn't yet quite forty, and the woman looked about thirty years old, although it was hard to tell through the overdone make-up.

"Two pints of Old Snoggins," Jonny said. "You'll like that one, it's the best they've got on at the moment."

When she had pulled the first pint, the woman placed the glass clumsily down in front of Peter, sloshing beer onto the towelling mat on the bar counter. Peter watched the head settle as she pulled Jonny's pint, and the beer was a good way short of the mark.

"Ain't you never satisfied," the woman said when Peter asked her to top up his glass.

When Jonny had paid, they crossed the room to a quiet corner table and sat down.

"Seven or eight years, that's a long time," Jonny said.

Around them the murmur of voices rose and fell, crisp packets crackled, glasses clinked, a few people came and went, one or two greeted Jonny as they passed. Early evening was a quiet time, but the pub would soon fill with people and the sound of merriment. One thing there wasn't was loud music, or any music at all. This chain prided itself on operating 'pubs where people can talk'—and that suited Peter very well.

"Yes, a long time," he said. "I don't know how it got to be so long, except I don't get back here much now that both my parents are dead. The last time I was here was for mum's funeral, and I had to leave straight after—two years ago that was."

"Well, however long it's been, it's really good to see you."

"And you, Jonny. But even now I can't stay long, and I can only drink one pint, because I have to drive back tonight."

"A shame you can't stay over, we could have got pie eyed, like in the old days."

Peter laughed.

"I wanted to give you something, Jonny." Peter's hand went to a jacket pocket, and came out with his fist clenched around something. He held his hand towards Jonny.

"Oh no," Jonny said, "not that old trick. You did that a lot when we were kids. Once you put a lump of dried dog shit into my hand, another time a slug. Do you remember?"

"I remember," Peter said, "but it's nothing like that."

"I don't trust you, not when it comes to this, you're too much of a prankster."

Peter laughed again.

"Put whatever it is on the table, so I can see it first."

When Jonny saw what it was, he stared in open-mouthed silence for what seemed, to Peter, like a long time.

"My God, it's Trooper Tommy," he said at last, his voice quiet, "it's Trooper Tommy. Where did you find him, Pete?"

Jonny picked up the lead soldier, turned it over and over between his fingers, smiled.

Peter remembered that Jonny had only ever called him Pete at the most solemn moments of their friendship. He smiled too, it was as if they were small boys again.

"It must be all of a quarter century since I saw Trooper Tommy. Where did you find him, Pete?"

"I went to the old house, Jonny, and I remembered about our camp, and I wondered if it was still there. And I went through the hedge, just like we used to. Look, stains on my jeans just like we always got." Peter pointed to his knees. "Then I was in our camp, I don't remember crawling through those bushes, and I was a boy again, and you were there and our treasure chest and we talked and played and planned just like we used to. Then your mum called you to go to the cinema, and I was alone and big again." The words gushed out of Peter as if he were a schoolboy telling his mother what he had done that day. Suddenly he felt embarrassed.

"Trooper Tommy," Jonny said, he smiled. "Thank you, Peter. It feels like a knot has been untangled inside me, a length of string has been straightened out to connect me to my past again. I haven't thought about those times for so long. Thank you."

They sat and slowly drank their beers. They talked about many things, they remembered and laughed and remembered some more. Finally it was time for Peter to leave.

"I'll walk to your car with you," Jonny offered.

And so they walked the narrow streets until they reached the car park. They saw half a dozen youths kicking a football about, their raucous voices bringing the street alive in the summer evening light. They saw old couples pottering out for a meal or to the pub or to evensong in the parish church, they saw shadows grow.

"I forgot to tell you," Peter said, "I saw Bobby Locke in the field, he still wants to bully, but he's too fat to do much now by the looks of him—he walks like a duck."

He thought he saw Jonny shudder at the mention of their nemesis, then they both laughed.

When he was in his car, Peter wound the window down to say goodbye to Jonny.

"Don't leave it so long before you come again."

"Why don't you come to London, I can put you up for a few nights."

Jonny nodded noncommittally.

"It was good to see you, Jonny, and your old man, he's looking very frail now, but we had a good chat over the garden fence—he gave me your phone number."

Peter turned the key in the ignition and the engine purred to life; his left hand went to adjust the mirror, more out of habit than necessity.

Jonny leaned towards the open window again.

"Pete," he said, "my dad died about four months ago, you couldn't have seen him, you couldn't have talked with him. It must have been a trick of memory."

Then Jonny turned and walked slowly away.

A shiver went down Peter's spine. He turned the engine off.

"Jonny," he called through the open window, "your dad gave me your phone number—he gave me your phone number."

But although the car park was quiet, Jonny didn't hear.

Stone

Cracked glass and cobwebs, broken roof tiles, fragments of domestic debris and the mushroomy smell of rotting wood, were what disagreeably confronted Robert Windlesham as he pushed open the door to his grandfather's old home.

He'd driven three hours to reach the cottage on a hillside, and if it hadn't been for the thought of the drive being pointless and the wasted time being doubled he would have immediately returned to his car and gone back to his home. Instead, he shrugged his shoulders and, knowing already that coming here was a mistake, entered the building he remembered from his childhood.

Only sunlight shafting through the damaged roof allowed him to see the sorry interior, the sad interior that had once been a happy and normal place. There were no echoes from the constant old-young laughter he remembered from his childhood, no consoling words, no comforting arms. There was no aroma of tobacco from a burning pipe, no log fire, no Bakelite radio tuned to a well-spoked BBC voice, no smiling, crinkled face. All that remained of the old man's life, apart from Robert's memories and a few photographs his mother had given him, were crunching fragments of willow pattern on the floor, scattered playing cards and yesterdays magazines.

Robert's mother had locked the cottage after her father's funeral, when the handful of mourners had sipped their sherry and drunk their tea and eaten their polite, vicarage sandwiches and left. That was twenty-five years ago, when Robert was still a teenager. She had intended to return to empty the place, to try to sell it, but everything she'd wanted to keep had already been removed, and as her sadness never left her she had never returned.

No one had been here since, apart from glue sniffers and drug users who'd left their paraphernalia here, ritualistically placed for later use, then abandoned as a testament to their wasted lives.

Now the future of these walls that had absorbed four generations of his family's secrets was in Robert's hands. He intended to sell the building, the land on which it stood and the stone-built shed near the tree-line that had been his grandfather's workshop. But being here, remembering, was draining the will to sell from him.

He moved through the desolation of the living room and kitchen. He went upstairs to bedrooms, furnished now only with the mementos of others who had stopped here for a while, the pungent smell of urine soaked mattresses and dead birds, the empty methylated spirits bottles, the remains of uneaten food not very old. He looked, he prodded with his feet, he opened cupboard doors, but there was nothing here he wanted to touch, nothing that held a memory. Downstairs again, he left the cottage and walked around the outside of the building.

Solid stone walls were solid still. Repairs had been made, but as his grandfather had been a mason, the workmanship was good. Somewhere, he recalled, was a stone on which his own birth had been commemorated by the old man, his name and a date precisely incised as only a trained hand could.

When Robert found the stone he traced the letters of his name with a finger and the date '7th June, 1970'. He'd forgotten he was almost forty-four years old and shuddered as he wondered where the years had gone.

His grandfather had been a monumental mason who mostly worked for undertakers, with occasional work on an historic property as a side-line. He had even carved his own simple gravestone in readiness; it bore his name, the year of his birth, a space for the year of his death to be incised by another, and the words 'An Honest Man'. When she saw the stone his mother had cried.

"It's true," she said to Robert between sobs, "it's true. Your grandpa was such an honest man."

Then she regained her composure and smiled at him. He never saw his mother cry again.

Robert returned to the rear of the cottage and walked across to his grandfather's workshop. Built from local stone it stood solid, windows were broken, but the door was still closed and even its roof appeared to have survived intact, perhaps due to the shelter afforded by the trees. Around the base of its walls piles of stone chippings were concealed by the encroachment of grass and weeds.

He felt closer to his grandfather here than he had in the desecrated cottage, and closing his eyes he imagined he could still hear the tap of a mason's mallet against a wood-handled chisel, the metal chisel blade chasing the stone, *tap-tap-tap-tapetty*, *tap-tap-tap-tapetty*, his grandfather's hacking cough. Here he felt haunted, truly haunted, and cliché though he knew it was, a chill jolted through him and, at that moment, a breeze sprang up and the branches overhead began to sough and creak.

Robert smiled rationally. He felt haunted, yes, but by memories, nothing more than memories, and the only thing that disturbed him was that he hadn't thought about his grandfather for so long. He'd spent many happy summers here as a child and remembered loving and trusting the incredibly old man without reservation.

When he was a teenager he'd seen his grandfather less often, but he still loved him, and after his mother told him that grandpa had died, he'd wept for hours when he thought of things not done and words not spoken. Now he was here to dispose of this part of his past and that was something at the moment he felt convinced he shouldn't do.

His thoughts focussed on returning to his car, parked on the hillside lane at the front of the property, and driving home. Perhaps he'd return another day, when the past wasn't so present and memories were less sharp, perhaps he wouldn't. He didn't need to sell, he didn't need the money, but had imagined that selling the cottage would simplify his life now that he had reached middle age. For the first time he was beginning to understand why his mother had never sold her childhood home.

He turned and started to walk away, then on impulse he returned to the building. Something deep inside told him he should take what might be his last look inside his grandfather's workshop.

He peered through the window, but could see little, so he tried the door. It yielded a little but didn't open. He pushed harder and it gave him only another inch. Finally he put his shoulder against the door and pushed with all his strength. Little by little, accompanied by the scraping of stone against stone, it moved inwards. When the door would move no farther there was an opening just large enough for him to squeeze into the room. A gravestone had fallen flat behind the door.

Robert bent over and used both hands to lift the stone upright. He dragged it farther into the workshop and leant it against the wall. Then he opened the door wide and could see his grandfather's array of tools neatly arranged on the workbench just as he remembered, the fallen gravestone had deterred looters for twenty-five years.

He closed his eyes again, just as he had outside, but could no longer hear the tap-tap-tap-tapetty, tap-tap-tap-tapetty of mallet against chisel and chisel against stone or the hacking cough of a dying man.

He looked at the gravestone he'd stood up, fascinated, he traced the inscription with a finger, just as he had with his name on the cottage wall. Suddenly, realising what the inscription said, he pulled his hand away from the stone and stepped quickly outside, slamming the door closed behind him. He heard the heavy sound of stone hitting stone, he heard the dragging sound of stone against stone.

He wanted to try the door again, but his mind was burning with denial, his face was dripping perspiration. He hurried to his car and climbed in. He started the engine, reached for a bottle of water he'd purchased when he'd filled the tank with petrol, drank it down swiftly. He pulled slowly away and just as slowly his inner turmoil abated.

A few miles away from the cottage his rational mind told him that he was mistaken about the gravestone inscription, but just as rationally he knew his finger hadn't lied.

Robert Windlesham
1970—2024
An Honest Man

Vinegar Hill

"Can you believe that we've lived here eight years already?" Alexa Burstwick said to her husband Carl. Her words were more a statement than a question, and the response she received was much as she expected, Carl grunted without looking up from his book.

She returned to her own book, but her thoughts were on the house now.

They'd been so lucky to purchase it at what they considered a bargain price. The selling agent told them it had seen seven owners in ten years, and that made buyers suspicious and the property harder to sell. They'd purchased from a middle aged couple, who cryptically wished them good luck when the deal was done. That had puzzled Alexa, but Carl always insisted that it meant nothing, it was just something for the other couple to say.

Built from smooth, red Victorian bricks in the 1890s, the house stood on a small rise beside the parish church in the centre of the village. It had been a rectory for what had then been the estate church of a local landowner, who had believed that building such a solid residence for a man of God would guarantee his entry into heaven, it had remained in use until the 1960s when the estate fell on hard times and the rectory was just another asset to be sold.

Alexa remembered that it had been their intention to use the large house as both a home and a business—a bed and breakfast. She had been pregnant with Benny at the time and had given up her job. The bed and breakfast had been her idea.

"I can work from home and look after the baby at the

same time," she'd said to Carl, and he agreed. Benny, at that time, didn't have a name, although they knew their child would be a boy; they hadn't yet decided between the six fashionably unfashionable names they'd shortlisted—Lucius, Albert, Benny, Kristoffer, Sebastian and Clovis.

Benny was born two months after they moved in, on exactly the day he was meant to arrive, while they were still decorating rooms, unpacking boxes and getting everything the way they wanted it to be.

Where those eight years had gone Alexa didn't know, but despite a few problems with Benny they'd been happy years; she knew that. Despite their best intentions the bed and breakfast had never happened. The discovered they liked rattling around in a six bedroom house. Large, but cosy, it had been thoughtfully triple glazed by an earlier owner, and the central heating was good.

Benny had been a strange child almost from the day of his birth. He rarely cried, rarely chuckled, and they both often saw his big, dark eyes staring intently at something they couldn't see. He was good through the night as well, at least until he was about two years old.

Then things began to change. He became reluctant to go to bed and he always wanted Alexa or Carl to sit with him until he fell asleep. His nights became restless, he often woke up screaming, and usually ended the night, for the sake of everyone, sleeping in his parents' bed.

After fifteen months, after numerous visits to their doctor and child sleep specialists, Benny's disturbed nights stopped. They stopped quite suddenly, and the family returned to quiet nights and restful sleep.

By the time Benny started attending the village school the teachers and other parents all said what a nice, happy boy he was. That made Alexa very proud. Her son was invited to birthday parties, he had friends over to play, and their large garden was often filled with the joyful sound of young children discovering themselves and the world.

"I'm going to bed, dear," she said to Carl, "don't be too long, it's getting late."

Carl looked up from his book, reached out, took her hand and kissed it.

"I'll be up as soon as you've warmed the bed for me," he said.

****

When Benny woke up in the night to sounds he had never heard before he pulled his bedsheet over his head and trembled in the darkness. They were insistent sounds that went on and on, something scratching at the wall behind his bed. As he trembled in his warm cocoon the sounds continued. Tears began to run across his cheeks. Eventually he screamed.

Within moments his father had noisily rattled the bedroom door open and entered, turning on the light as he came.

"What is it, Benny? What's the matter son? Did you have a nightmare?"

As his room was flooded with light, Benny came out from under the sheet and saw the familiar curtains with their pattern of smiling steam engines, the wallpaper printed with cartoon characters, the shelf with annuals, that grew a little fuller every Christmas, and the toys he loved perched on every available surface. Everything was so normal, so as it should be, and the scratching sounds had stopped.

He saw too, his father's face, smiling reassuringly.

Carl sat on the edge of the bed, took Benny in his arms and held him close. Smelling of sleep and perspiration, making soothing noises, the familiar presence comforted Benny and his sobbing gradually subsided.

"It wasn't a nightmare, daddy, I heard something and I was frightened."

"What did you hear Benny? Tell me about it. I'm sure it was nothing really."

Benny knew that nothing scary in the night was real to grown-ups. Nothing frightened them.

His mother had appeared in the doorway, she was smiling.

"Tell daddy about it, Benny, there's a good boy." Alexa said in a soothing voice.

"Something was scratching on the wall—here," Benny's words were hesitant, tentative; he stretched out a small arm and pointed to a cartoon cowboy.

"Let's take a look, shall we," Carl said. He sat Benny on the bed, stood up and then moved to pull the bed a few inches away from the wall. "There's no sign of any scratching, son, no sign at all. Can you see?"

Benny reluctantly nodded his head.

"I think it was coming from inside the wall, daddy."

"It's a solid wall, son, nothing could be inside that." As he spoke he thumped on the papered surface with his fist. "See, as solid as rock."

"You imagined it dear," Alexa said, "you had a bad dream, that's all. Try to go back to sleep now, we'll leave the light on outside your door and the door open, but just a tiny bit."

She crossed to his bedside, hugged him, kissed him, and tucked him in beneath a sheet so tight he could barely move.

"Goodnight, Benny, we love you," they said in unison as they left his room.

****

At breakfast, Benny was listless and didn't chatter away as he usually did—asking why about anything that crossed his mind or telling his parents the latest playground joke. He had been unable to sleep after his parents had left, and for three hours or more he'd returned to hiding beneath his bedsheet.

"You look tired, Benny." His mother said as she put a glass of milk in front of him.

"I didn't sleep no more."

"Any more, not no more," her words of correction were routine, delivered without a thought, "were you still worried by your nightmare?"

"The scratching sounds kept me awake."

"We agreed that was just a bad dream, Benny, didn't we!"

"Yes, mummy, but they were real sounds, honestly they were, and they got louder."

****

That was the first night Benny heard the scratching sounds. He was nine years old. They continued night after night, except for a couple of nights one or other of his parents spent in his room with him—and heard nothing.

For the first few months he was a very miserable, very tired little boy. His school work suffered badly, his friends laughed at him when he told them about the sounds. He felt totally alone.

In his mind he began to construct an explanation for what he was hearing.

He decided that a secret person lived in the walls. He thought it was a girl as old as he was, and the scratching sounds she made were messages to him that he could not understand. He called her Anne. With the sounds personified he gradually stopped being worried by them. He still woke up to them almost every night, but he would say 'I don't understand, Anne. I'm sorry.', and then he would go back to sleep. He never mentioned Anne to his parents, and the subject of the sounds didn't crop up again until he was fourteen years old.

Carl and Alexa agreed it was just a phase he went through, just as he'd been through phases of disturbed nights before. The needed no more explanation, and family life continued in the happy way they'd become accustomed to. They hadn't mentioned the bed and breakfast for years, but in four or five years Benny would be off to university, then, they thought, then they might finally start their own small business.

****

Benny had done his homework and was stretched out on his bed with his iPod plugged into his ears when his mother came into his room.

"I did knock, but you didn't hear me with those things stuck in your ears. You'll go deaf you know."

"What do you want mum?" Benny sighed. "I finished my homework."

"Don't be irritable with me. I want to tell you something." She paused, as if expecting Benny to say something, but he stayed silent. "Do you remember those sounds you said you used to hear in the wall behind your bed? Well, I was in here this morning tidying up your mess, and I could swear I heard a scratching sound."

"A…," Anne, Benny started to say, but managed to make it sound like 'ah', "just a bad dream mum… or a bad daydream."

Alexa smiled and they both laughed.

"I just thought you'd like to know that I can imagine things every bit as well as you can."

She turned to leave the room and then paused. When she looked at Benny he was fumbling the buds of his iPod into his ears again. In the silence she heard scritt scritt scritt, scritt scritt scritt, coming from the wall behind Benny's bed. The sound terrified her in its quiet way, it was real, but for Benny's sake she managed to remain calm.

"Listen," she said, "do you here that? I hear it."

Benny disconnected from his iPod again, glared at his mother and listened. He heard the familiar sound of Anne sending her messages through the wall.

"It's real, isn't it Benny?"

"Yes mum, it's real. But it's nothing to worry about. I'm used to it by now. I call her Anne."

"Her? I'm so sorry Benny, so sorry we didn't believe you."

"No harm done mum, look at me—perfectly normal."

His mother looked worried, but she smiled anyway.

"I'm not so sure about 'normal'."

****

When Benny's father got home from work, the three of them sat and talked about the scratching sounds. Every time Benny said the name Anne, they looked disconcerted but went along with it.

"I'm glad she let mum hear her, even if it did take her nearly six years." Benny said after his father had gone to listen and returned declaring that he'd heard nothing out of the ordinary.

"It's probably just a mouse under the floorboards or something."

"That's no mouse, dad."

"He's right," Alexa said, "it's far too loud to be a mouse, and it's in the wall not under the floor."

"We'll call someone in to investigate—though I can't imagine that's a cavity wall, why would it be, it's internal?"

"This house is more than a century old, you can't know how they built in those days. Not like now, I'm sure." Alexa said reproachfully.

His father grunted, and none of them said any more on the subject.

****

"Did you really hear scratching sounds from that wall?" Carl asked Alexa just before they went to bed that night.

"I certainly did," Alexa tried not to show her irritation at Carl's question. "First in the daytime when I was tidying up, and again this evening not long before you got home. I was really frightened, but Benny was so blasé about it—imagine how frightened he must have been when he was little, and we didn't even believe him."

"Young kids imagine things; we weren't to know."

In the darkened room Alexa glared at her husband, but she said nothing and they both drifted off to sleep.

****

"You want me to examine a wall to see if there's anything wrong with it," the local builder said when he arrived at the house on Saturday morning.

"Something like that," Carl replied. "You'll need some tools, a heavy hammer, a chisel. I want you to remove a couple of bricks so we can see if an internal wall is a cavity wall."

"It won't be, mate, they never are."

"Will you check anyway?"

"I'll do what you like, you're the one who's paying me."

He returned to his Transit van and returned with his tools.

"Show me the wall."

All four of them made their way to Benny's bedroom. His disassembled bed and its mattress were leaning against a hall wall and they had to squeeze past.

166

"This wall," Benny's father said, "remove a couple of bricks about here." He patted the spot, low down, about the level Benny's mattress would be. "My wife and son have both heard scratching sounds coming from the wall."

"This ain't no bloody cavity wall, but it's your money, and it will ruin…"

"Just remove the bricks, please, the room is due to be done anyway—redecorated I mean."

Peeling away an area of wallpaper as best he could, the builder began to chip away at the layer of plaster beneath. Little by little an area of brickwork was revealed.

"There's something funny here mate. I'd say this house is late Victorian, but see these bricks here, they're much older."

"Early Victorian?" Benny's father asked.

"Much older. I'd guess these are from the sixteenth or seventeenth century. You can tell in my work. They're hand-made for a start, and the size gives them away too. I don't know if I should remove them, they might be protected."

"Just two or three please—I'll pay you more."

At the mention of more pay the builders eyes glinted and he began to scrape away mortar between two courses of bricks.

****

Within forty minutes four bricks had been removed and were resting among the debris on the bedroom carpet. Behind where they had been was blackness that not even light coming through the window wanted to penetrate.

"Blow me, that's a cavity right enough, you were right mate." The builder leaned forward and tried to see what was inside.

"Apart from it stinks in there, I can't see nothing."

"Anything not nothing," Alexa automatically corrected.

"What was that, lady?" The builder asked.

"Oh, nothing, I was talking to my son," she replied as both she and Benny stifled laughter.

"Have you got a torch?"

"I'll get one." Benny left the room and quickly returned with a rubber-cased torch from the kitchen.

Shining the beam into the cavity the builder peered again.

"No good," he said. "The light just vanishes after an inch or two as if it's being swallowed by the dark.

"It's the most powerful one we've got, and anyway, how can dark swallow light, that's a silly idea," Carl said. "Let me look."

He knelt beside the builder, took the torch and shone it into the cavity as he leaned forward and peered. "He's right, the light doesn't penetrate far enough—and it does stink, not like mould or mildew, but as if something's gone bad."

"I'll stick me arm in and see how far back this goes." After only seconds the builder withdrew his dust and cobweb covered arm. "Eighteen inches or so I'd guess. That's a big cavity and it's very cold in there. I felt something too, like an old pipe or something. What's the next room?"

"Bathroom," the three of them chorused.

"But there are no pipes through that wall," Benny's father added.

Pushing his arm into the hole again the builder felt around.

"Not pipes," the builder said, "too irregular even for old pipes. We'll soon see what this is." He almost fell backwards as he tugged at something and it gave way.

When he fully withdrew his arm he looked at what he was holding, and then quickly dropped it. He scrambled to his feet and brushed the dust and cobwebs from his arm.

"I reckons that's bone, mate. Bone is what it is." He collected his tools back into their bag. "You don't owe me for this, nothing, but you gotta call the coppers. Someone dead's in there." Then he rushed downstairs, slammed the door as he left the house and drove off in his Transit.

****

Six months later the Burstwicks received a visit from the police inspector who'd come to investigate the macabre find in Benny's bedroom.

"I thought you should know," he said, "the bones you found in your wall were of a young woman, maybe eighteen or twenty years old. We reckon she was bricked up there at least two-hundred and fifty years ago. It's a historical crime, there's no chance of catching the one who did that to her. It seems your house was built around what remained of a much older house that the landowner wouldn't allow to be demolished. Every trace of that building was concealed."

"What happens now?" Carl asked.

"Nothing really, sir. The girl's bones will be given a Christian burial in the churchyard next door. It's where the poor lass belongs. There will be a short funeral service, you can attend if you wish. I'll let you know when it is."

"We'll come," Alexa said. "We owe her that much."

"I want to go too," Benny added.

Alexa smiled.

****

Benny's bedroom was redecorated after the cavity was sealed again. The Burstwicks weren't allowed to demolish the old wall, and the whole building was given grade two listed status. Benny moved to another room while the work was done, and never returned to his old room. Unused, seldom entered, it was like a shrine to his childhood and a memorial to Anne all in one.

Members of the local historical society became interested in the house when they read press reports of what had been discovered there, and were disappointed that there was nothing interesting for them to see when Alexa agreed to let a small party of them visit.

They drank tea and ate biscuits as they muttered 'so ordinary, so ordinary' among themselves.

****

On the first Sunday morning after Anne's funeral Benny appeared late for breakfast.

"You look tired," Carl said as Alexa tended bacon that was sizzling nicely under the grill.

"I didn't sleep well," Benny said.

"Too much on your mind?"

Benny was reluctant to say any more, but both parents were concerned that he had slept badly.

"I heard scratching noises coming from the wall," he said in a hushed voice, "really I did."

Three days later the agents erected a 'For Sale' sign outside Vinegar Hill—or 'that house' as local people now called it.

Mr & Mrs Pewsey

Mr Pewsey had no interest in lepidoptery, other than knowing that Cabbage Whites were regular pests in his summertime garden, and it wasn't a Cabbage White that was trailing after him. He was accustomed to strange things happening to him, so that morning, as he wandered idly towards the churchyard, he paid no attention to the butterfly that followed along behind.

It was a pleasant morning and he enjoyed the weekly routine of visiting Mrs Pewsey's grave. He enjoyed tugging out the weeds that had grown around her. He enjoyed snipping at the already short grass with the kitchen scissors he always took with him—although he tried to leave the daisies, because Mrs Pewsey liked daisies, she always used to say that they reminded her of tiny fried eggs. He enjoyed replacing the withered flowers with the fresh ones he'd picked while they were still speckled with morning dew. He enjoyed the conversations that maintained the love they had shared through fifty-seven years of marriage. He often thought that it was as if his Mrs Pewsey wasn't really dead at all.

As he pushed open the lychgate its rusted hinges groaned, just as they always did, the sound they made was the accompaniment to his visits here. It was harsh and grating and it helped call him back from whatever flight of fancy his mind had taken up. He could never remember where those imaginary journeys had carried him, what he had seen, what he had done, but they were always gone as soon as the lychgate opened. His ability to recall hadn't always been so bad.

"I must oil those hinges, I must. Good morning Mr Pewsey."

It always puzzled Mr Pewsey as to why the vicar should mention oiling hinges every time they met, no matter where it was. It was just another strange occurrence he decided. He expected to hear the vicar's voice today, but the Reverend Dorchester was nowhere to be seen and that was good. He'd always found him to be an excessively emollient man with a calculating manner.

He walked along the path towards the church—a stocky, Norman affair with a stump of a tower at one end. He'd never thought it an attractive building, but its great age meant it couldn't possibly be ugly. His wife's grave was at the rear and he liked to walk the path that encircled the church and run his hands across the weathered stones. He felt their antiquity tingle into him and for some reason that made him feel younger, more alive. He never ceased to marvel at the tool marks still visible on the surface of the stone, a reminder of men with unknown lives but whose signatures in stone would never fade.

Mrs Pewsey's headstone was simple. A simple headstone for an extraordinary woman, he'd decided, it's what she would have wanted. What made her extraordinary? He thought it was the fact that she'd stayed with him for fifty-seven years—sixty-one years if you counted the years of their courting. They'd been eighteen years old when they met. Their mothers had become friends while their fathers were away fighting in the war.

Doris Pewsey
Darling wife
She lived a full and loving life
and will always be missed

Mr Pewsey knelt on the grass beside his wife's grave. It always seemed disrespectful, to him, to kneel on the grave itself. He was glad to see that the weeds he'd pulled on his last visit hadn't grown again. Should he cut the grass or not? He ran his hand across it and decided it could be left for another week—that would give them more time to talk. He removed the withered flowers from the stone vase embedded in the ground in front of the headstone and replaced them with the fresh flowers he'd carried here. Their bright reds and yellows and blues contrasted so well with the grey of the stone and the green of the grass.

As he was arranging the flowers, a thrush alighted on the headstone, unconcerned by his presence, and trilled its merry song. That's so beautiful, Mr Pewsey thought, Doris will like that.

"It *is* beautiful, dear," Doris Pewsey said.

"Yes, yes it is," Mr Pewsey replied.

It didn't seem at all strange to him that he could talk with his dead wife. Strange things happened to him often, and on his measure of strangeness talking to Doris was quite normal.

"How have you been, Bernard? Have you been well?"

"I think I've been well, Doris, as far as I can say."

"That's good dear. You now you must look after yourself."

"I will."

"The flowers are lovely. I really look forward to your visits and the new flowers you bring."

"I look forward to my visits too."

As the sun rose higher into the sky, Bernard could feel its warmth through his jacket. Doris had always joked with him about the way he always wore a jacket, even on the warmest, sunniest of days. Bees and other insects were attracted to the bright flowers he had brought, he found their soft noises very soothing as he knelt there, he knew that Doris enjoyed their music as well.

"I miss you so very much Doris," Bernard said. "Being here with you makes it seem as if you are still here."

"I will always be with you my darling, you know that. I will always be in your heart just as you will always be in mine."

"Do the children ever visit you? Peter, Susan, do they ever come here?"

"Never, they never come. I think they've forgotten me, but I don't mind, they have their lives to live and our grandchildren to care for."

"I suppose so. They never visit me either."

"Why can't we be together?" They both asked.

When they spoke those words in unison their laughter fell

like cherry blossom and cheered them both. Bernard realised that neither of them really minded the children not visiting. Life moved on, the new always displaced the old, the young always displaced the old too.

They talked some more, shared long-forgotten memories awakened by being together. Bernard hummed Doris' favourite song for her. Then, after a period—that could have been minutes or hours—when it was enough just to share silence with his beloved, it was time for him to leave.

"I must go now my love," he said to Doris.

"Yes, you must go. Take care my dear, dear husband. Come again. . . soon."

"I will," Bernard said as he struggled to his feet, "I will."

As he reached the corner of the church, he turned and blew Doris a kiss. He knew how much she liked that.

He walked through the village, passed the busy shops, passed the busy people. No one recognised him, no one spoke to him. He wondered when life had become so urgent, so much to be rushed. He came to the Royal Oak, his favourite pub, and thought about having a pint, but it was only a thought.

At the edge of the village he came to the cottage hospital. Doris had spent time in there, and so had he. Peter and Susan had both been born there, but that was a long time ago.

Beyond the hospital he reached home.

He walked between the tall, brick-built gate-posts. The fragrance of flowers was everywhere, the sun still shone brightly, it was a perfect day. He crossed the well cut grass, stopping now and then to remember a friend, an acquaintance. By and by he reached his grave. There were no fresh cut flowers for him, no manicured grass, but he didn't mind, Doris was happy, and that's what mattered... that was all that mattered. He would never understand why he was in the town cemetery and Doris was in the churchyard. Why couldn't they be together? It would have been so right.

Snow

When Mrs Dorry reached the kitchen and saw snow drifting past the window, she immediately called to her husband.

"David, David, it's snowing… do you think…"

"I hate the bloody snow," David called back. "I have to be out there driving in it, while you can stay snug and warm at home."

Even David's grumpiness didn't put an end to Mrs Dorry's joy at seeing snow. She peered out through the window, she watched the snowflakes doing their random dance as they fell to the ground. She watched and watched. She forgot to make the coffee or to prepare David's toast, the only breakfast he would ever eat, as he got ready to go to work.

"Where's my breakfast?" David asked as he came into the kitchen. He was neatly dressed in the smart uniform provided by the courier company he worked for, his dark blue tie was correctly knotted and he had tough, waterproof boots on his feet. "Where's the coffee."

"Sorry, dear," Mrs Dorry said brightly, "I'll make your coffee and toast right now. I was watching the snow, you know why, do you think…"

"I know why," he replied, "and it's nonsense, you know it is. I'll be late if you make breakfast now." With that he headed for the door, without even giving his wife her customary kiss on the cheek.

"Sorry, dear," Mrs Dorry said again.

"If this snow keeps falling, I'll be late tonight." Then David opened the door, stepped outside, and closed the door much more noisily than he should have.

Mrs Dorry felt the wintry air that rushed into the kitchen, and she felt her husband's displeasure too. She missed his kiss on the cheek, even though she knew it meant little. They both knew that there wasn't much love left in their marriage, the best that could be said for them is that they were comfortable together. They'd discussed getting a divorce once, but that had been years ago, and they'd agreed that there wasn't much point in doing that as they approached sixty, neither of them wanted to grow old and be lonely. She shrugged her shoulders, dabbed a solitary tear from the corner of her right eye, and went back to watching the snow.

She could see David's footprints going along the path towards the garage at the end of the garden, he'd started the car already. She could see a cloud of exhaust fumes rising above the hedge that kept all but the garage roof from being seen from the kitchen. It hadn't been snowing long because the path carried only a thin covering of snow. She so hoped it would continue snowing for a good part of the day… she really hoped that.

After making herself a small pot of tea, she carried it and all the paraphernalia, cup and saucer, milk jug, teaspoon, no sugar, on a tray to the living room of their bungalow. On the way, she stopped to turn the central heating thermostat up a degree or two. David would appreciate the extra warmth tonight.

She placed her tray on the coffee-table, poured her tea, and then sat in an armchair from which she had a good view of the falling snow.

After a while, to her staring eyes, the steady procession of snowflakes had a hypnotic effect on Mrs Dorry. Individual flakes became moments from her life, fragments of memories, a harsh word from someone, a kind word from someone else. She recalled things she'd owned, but no longer owned, things she'd yearned for that had never come her way. She recalled her life with David as well… for almost forty years they'd been together. Where had all those minutes and seconds gone, she wondered.

For a long time they had loved one another, for many years in fact, but one night, or so it seemed to her, that love had quietly gone away. She knew it wasn't her fault, just as she knew it wasn't David's fault. There was no blame to be shared, it had just happened. She knew exactly when it had happened. I was in the early summer, six months after… after…

She reached for her tea and sipped it. She was hungry, but even the thought of taking breakfast now was too much trouble.

She knew it was six months after Mary died. Every time it snowed she thought of her daughter. In fact she thought of Mary often, but especially, more meaningfully, when it snowed. Snow reminded her of Mary because the last time their child had played happily in the garden it had snowed heavily. David had gone to work, just as he had today, and Mary, nine-year-old Mary, had wanted to build a snowman. She had dressed her daughter warmly, right down to the pink, My Little Pony wellington boots she loved, and let her out into the front garden.

She'd watched from this very window as, little by little, Mary had gathered snow using her seaside bucket and spade, until she had a pile that was as tall as she was. She'd run to the living room window looking very proud, pressed her nose against the cold glass, and smiled at her mother.

"Mummy, mummy, come and help me," Mary had called.

Together they'd finished making the snowman. They made a large snowball for his head, used a carrot for his nose and pebbles for his eyes.

"He's cold, mummy, Snowie's cold," Mary had said. She was right, of course, how could a snowman not be cold?

When David came home from work, the three of them had stood by the living room window, looking out at Snowie as he glowed in the cold moonlight, a woollen scarf about his neck, an old hat upon his head.

Later, when they went to bed, David had peeped into Mary's room.

"She's fast asleep," he'd said, "I bet she's dreaming of Snowie, she really loves him you know."

"Yes," she'd replied, "she is so proud of him."

Next morning they had found Mary dead in her bed. No medical reason for her sudden death had ever been established, it was as if, they were told, she had just stopped working. Mrs

Dorry sobbed as she remembered this, twenty years ago it had been, and every time it snowed she cried a little.

Her tea was cold, and she wondered whether to make a fresh pot, but instead she returned to gazing at the snow. It was falling more heavily now, and she knew David would be in a foul mood when he returned home. She decided to make him a special dinner, but it was far too early to start that now. So she watched the snow.

She remembered that it was the winter two years after Mary died that she returned for the first time. Mrs Dorry had been doing the things she did, tidying the bungalow, making their bed, doing the laundry. Mid-morning, she decided to have coffee. She had carried it through to the living room, just as she had her tea, she had sat in the same chair. She'd looked up at the slate-grey sky, she'd said 'snow' to herself. Soon it was snowing heavily. The garden was covered in no time, and the snow was soon a couple inches deep.

Then, as she watched, something that she called 'a little whirlwind' had formed, it turned and turned, not quickly, not slowly, and at its centre a pile of snow grew until it was about three feet high.

Mrs Dorry knew it was Mary. What else could it be? She didn't know how she knew, and she told herself she didn't need to know how she knew. She rushed to the front door, opened it and peered out.

"Mary," she called tentatively, "is that you darling?"

As if responding to her voice, the 'little whirlwind' moved a few feet towards her, she felt the cold draught from its whirling.

"Mary?" She said again. "Darling?"

Mrs Dorry swore to herself afterwards that the whirlwind had sighed, it sound like a word elongated and whispered, it sounded like 'mummy'.

Then the whirlwind vanished, and the column of snow collapsed into a small mound.

By the time David arrived home, she felt real joy in her heart. She'd made the special meal, they'd even opened a bottle of wine, and David mellowed.

"Something happened today," she said.

Then she told David about the little whirlwind and the column of snow and the sigh that sounded like 'mummy'.

David became angry.

"You know this is nonsense, it's ridiculous," and he'd stormed from the kitchen to the living room, where he played a country music CD very loudly.

Mrs Dorry had cried as she washed the dishes, but she told herself over and over, 'it was Mary, it was Mary'.

Now each winter, when the snow comes, just as it has today, she sits and she watches, she sits and she waits.

Sometimes, but not always, she sees a little whirlwind. She sees a column of snow grow on the lawn until it is about three feet high.

She feels tears run down her cheeks.

She wants to open the front door and speak Mary's name, but she doesn't want to frighten her little whirlwind away, so she just watches.

She says to herself 'Mary, Mary, Mary', and she knows joy.

She tells David nothing of this, because she knows David wouldn't understand.

Elements

Earth

Oliver had been obsessed with being thought of as a good man ever since his youth. Before he was old enough to vote he'd joined a voluntary organization that looked after the gardens of those who could no longer manage for themselves. This choice, in a way, determined the course of his life.

Academically bright, instead of going to a conventional university and becoming a historian or a geographer, he'd opted instead to attend an agricultural college, taking horticultural courses in particular. He learned all about plants, their seasons, and how to keep a garden looking colourful at any time of year. By the time he graduated he already had a guaranteed position as an under-gardener at a stately home where he'd helped out during his summer breaks.

Palace House, Beaulieu, was, among the great stately homes; on the small side to be sure, but to him it was exquisite. Whereas the larger stately homes often verged on the ostentatious and displayed a vulgarity that was almost tawdry, Beaulieu was still like a real family home. Its owner, Lord Montagu, could often be found mingling with the tourists who went to visit the house or the extensive collection of vintage cars in the nearby Motor Museum.

One morning, Lord Montagu greeted his new gardener in the formal garden. His Lordship was a friendly man who carried his lineage with casual ease and had no need of airs and graces. He offered his hand for Oliver to shake, as soiled as Oliver's hands were, and asked him what his ambition was. Oliver thought for a moment before replying.

"I think my ambition is to be remembered as a good man, Your Lordship," he said.

Lord Montagu looked puzzled; then he smiled, instructed Oliver to keep up the good work, thanked him and walked on.

Oliver remained at Palace House for almost seven years. During that time, he learned the practical side of garden design, as well as all the tricks of the gardening trade. He felt, at last that he was ready to make his way in the world as a hands-on garden designer. In his mind he was convinced that those of lesser means than Lord Montagu would pay handsomely to have their gardens redesigned by someone who had been a gardener for His Lordship.

As things turned out, he was right. He had done very well for himself, he owned a nice house, a nice car (as well as his business vehicles) and took holidays in interesting places; but he had never married and had no children. Now he thought he was too old to marry and raise a family. Instead he fulfilled himself by doing good things, but in a very discreet way.

He supported local charities for the disabled, the blind and the homeless, each of which was delighted to receive quite large donations from a mysterious benefactor several times a year. He remembered how his own parents had struggled, and anonymously replaced worn out household appliances for poor families of the town. Women cried when a new washing machine or cooker arrived unexpectedly at their doors. He anonymously organised and paid for a day trip to the seaside each summer for children from the orphanage. He felt proud of these achievements. He was being a good man.

A few friends knew of his largesse and often asked him why he didn't use his money to buy a villa on the Mediterranean coast or a hideaway in Florida.

"I have everything I want here. I don't need to own a house in the sun to take a good holiday. My home is comfortable. I even have a swimming-pool and a real home-cinema room with comfortable seats and a giant screen. What more do I want.

Doing good for the benefit of others is my pleasure, so I'm being quite selfish when I help the needy. I like doing good. I want to be remembered as a good man."

As the years passed, his fortune grew; the money he didn't use to do good, he invested wisely. He built a chain of garden centres that were phenomenally successful, he developed and sold his own varieties of popular plants; but despite his business success his real work was still gardening. None of his clients knew that he was a multi-millionaire businessman when he dug trenches, hefted rocks around and cut down trees in their gardens—he was just Oliver, the garden designer and gardener who had been recommended to them.

There came a time in Oliver's life when his age touched sixty, just as it does for most of us. He began to take stock of his life, he examined his success, thought deeply about his good works, and wondered if he had really been good enough. He tried to think of new ways to do good, and worried when he had no ideas.

To take his mind off this problem, he picked up the latest package from the Forgotten Films Club; he'd been a member ever since he'd set up his home cinema. The club, as its name suggested, specialised in films that were forgotten, because most of them weren't very good. But occasionally he watched one that he thought was a real gem. This month's selection was *Walter: the Story of a Life*; it had been made in 1954 and Oliver had never heard of the director or any of the cast. At the end of the film a shadowy and indistinct figure watched a group of people in what appeared to be beautiful, wide-lawned parkland.

Walter was a successful businessman who became obsessed with the need to do good, and, as he watched, Oliver recognised that his own life mirrored that of Walter in many, many ways. Walter's solution for dealing with his large fortune was to set up a charitable foundation—emulating that became Oliver's big idea.

Over the next several weeks, Oliver discussed his idea with his financial adviser, his banker and his lawyer, all of whom thought it was a bad idea. Their reaction proved to him that setting up the Good Man Charitable Foundation had to be his priority. Supporting, in perpetuity, the causes that he already supported anonymously, was to be the main objective of his foundation. Oliver realised, however, that the many hundreds of millions he had invested would generate more than enough income for that, so his foundation was to have the freedom to seek new groups of people to help, provided only that the foundation's choices were compatible with the principles he would enshrine in its constitution.

All of Oliver's investments were transferred to the Good Man Charitable Foundation, a board of trustees was appointed and staff hired to manage the charity. He retained control of his businesses for the time being, although that too would pass to his foundation upon his death.

He continued to live as a very wealthy man for almost twenty years, and still had sufficient funds to commit to individual acts of kindness. His foundation grew into a behemoth among charities, and its helping hands encircled the globe. As he monitored its progress, without interfering, he felt very proud. He felt, in fact, that he had at last achieved that great and good thing for which he had been born among men. When that thought registered, Oliver breathed his last and died peacefully in his sleep.

His funeral service was a humanist one; there were none of the trappings of religion. His coffin, on his instructions, was made of sturdy cardboard that would quickly rot away in the ground. While still alive he'd purchased a field adjacent to the local cemetery, and had designed and landscaped it as a garden of peace where anyone could sit in silent contemplation. A corner of that garden was Oliver's final resting place on earth.

No mausoleum was to be raised to commemorate his life and good works and his grave marker was to be a simple granite slab. What was inscribed on that slab, if anything, Oliver left to others. His final wish had been for his coffin to be aligned so that his face looked towards a tree covered rise a short distance away.

Looking down from that rise was a shadowy and indistinct figure among the trees. It watched a small gathering of invitees with bowed heads around the grave. It couldn't hear the words spoken by the speaker, but hoped they were simple words. After a few minutes, those around the grave each picked up a handful of soil and let it trickle through their fingers onto the simple coffin. Then they moved slowly away. The figure watched as the gravediggers shovelled the mound of earth back into the hole. When that was finished, they moved a slab of stone into place; it was wider than the grave itself and was supported by the solid ground on either side. Their work finished, the two men moved off to dig another hole or mow the cemetery lawns or whatever else gravediggers did when not digging graves.

That was the end of Oliver—but for one last thing. From among the trees the shadowy and indistinct figure drifted down to the graveside. It was Oliver of course, or a version of him. He looked down at his grave marker and read the words inscribed there:

Oliver ———

1959—2039

A Good Man

He was pleased with the words, very pleased, proud even—but he found the gilt with which they were lined both showy and inappropriate.

Air

When she was growing up, Sarah loved the outdoors. She spent so much time among the trees in the large garden of her family home, that her mother told her that she should have been born as one of the woodland folk. She'd had no idea what that meant when she was seven or eight years old; the only woodland folk she knew of were in the stories in her colourful childhood books. They were small, happy people whose clothing was made from flower petals and leaves. They wore acorn cups as hats. Even the adult woodland folk spent most of their time playing among the trees with their friends the birds and butterflies.

As she grew older she realised that the woodland folk weren't real, that there was no fairyland utopia among the trees and no place were laws were not necessary because everyone was so honest and nice. By the time she was old enough to go into town by herself, her mother had warned her of darker things: don't walk through the woods if the sun isn't shining, never tread on someone else's shadow, never, ever talk to strangers, don't breathe in another's breath. She laughed, and told her mother not to worry, told her that she would be careful. In reality, though, she did just as all teenagers everywhere do, and that was exactly what she wanted. She walked through the woods rain or shine, because it was the shortest route to the bus stop; she trod on the shadows of others because it seemed silly to avoid doing so, she talked to strangers—especially if they were cute boys.

She always thought the prohibition on talking to strangers was a bit silly. If you never talk to strangers, she reasoned, you would only ever talk to your own family, you would never have friends or meet anyone new. She never said this to her mother, of course. Had she done so, she would have been punished for being rude or cheeky. Her mother had been very strict with her once her father had left. When he lived with them, he had managed to control her mother's anger and she had rarely been punished.

"You will understand one day, Sarah, and that's enough. Don't ask me about it again," her mother had said when Sarah asked why daddy wasn't at home any more.

She didn't see her father again until she was fifteen, and even then it was in secret. She saw a man waiting by the school gate, and she recognised him instantly. Her memory of him hadn't dimmed in the seven years since they'd last been together. Then he had just been daddy. Now, as she rushed towards him, arms outstretched, she thought he looked quite handsome.

"Who's this then, Sarah?" one of her school friends asked with a wink that might have been interpreted as having salacious intent.

"It's my da… it's my father, I mean."

"I didn't think you had a father."

"Of course I have a father, stupid. Everyone has a father somewhere—or had a father," she suddenly remembered that her friend's mother had been widowed two years earlier.

Her father was smiling in the way she remembered, with deep lines from the corners of his nose to the corners of his wide, red-lipped mouth. She wrapped her arms around him, hugged him and began to cry.

"Daddy, daddy, daddy," she sobbed over and over. "Where were you daddy? Where were you?"

It was as if she was a child again. She felt the warmth of his body through his clothing, felt his strength. His arms went around her, hugged her as she hugged him. She reached up and stroked his cheek, felt the stubble of his beard. She looked at his face, and saw his smiling eyes, they glistened with tears that didn't flow. She felt his warm breath against her cheek and breathed deeply of it.

As she was lost in welcoming her father back into her life she lost track of her homeward routine. She forgot there was a bus to catch and friends to laugh and joke with. Someone called her name, but it was distant, disconnected, meant for another Sarah, not the Sarah she was at that moment. Someone walked quickly by, brushed against her, grabbed her arm in passing. Sarah stumbled as she was pulled, let go of her father and turned, surprised to see the school bus waiting, its engine running.

"Quick… the bus," a voice said, it was her best friend.

Sarah was unwillingly pulled along. When she twisted her head to look back, her father was gone.

"Who was that old man you were cuddling? Too old for you, must be a perv."

"He's not old and he's my dad. And I wasn't cuddling him, I was hugging him." She was sure there was a difference between cuddling and hugging, but she wouldn't have been able to explain what it was.

When she reached home, she didn't mention to her mother that she had seen her father.

She knew that was a shortcut to a row, and the happiness inside her didn't want a row tonight. Her mother had prepared a make-do meal, from odds and ends left over from other meals, she was lucky to get even that. It was date night and soon her mother would be gone, she would be left alone to do whatever she wanted. She had homework, but when that was done all she wanted to do was think about her dad.

Somehow she knew he was there with her, in the very air she breathed. She could still smell him, still feel him. Without knowing why, she began to sob, but they were happy tears she was shedding. She was happy. She was happy. She had found her father.

Over the next two years she hugged her father a few more times outside the school gates. He was just there as she rushed towards the bus. She stopped, they hugged for what seemed like ages. His solidity, his hands, the air around him were all building blocks of her happiness. She moved towards the bus. When she looked he was gone. It was always like that. It didn't seem odd to her that they never spoke to each other. Such was the love she felt, from her to him, from him to her, that words didn't seem necessary.

At home, her life had become almost unbearably miserable; rows with her mother, rows with Piggy, her mother's boyfriend Roland, whose nickname came from his greed. To Sarah, it seemed that her presence in the house was something they didn't want, she was tolerated due to whatever sense of duty her mother still felt.

After one particularly bad row, Sarah, feeling that she could no longer tolerate her situation, stuffed a few things into a backpack and headed for the door.

"I'm off," she said. "You'll see me when you see me, if ever, that is."

"Don't you talk to me like that, young lady," her mother screeched, as Piggy held her at the waist from behind and smirked as he kissed her neck. "Where are you going?"

From the doorstep, Sarah looked back.

"I'm going to stay with dad. I've been meeting him for two years or more." she blurted out without really meaning to. She had no idea where her father lived.

Her mother's face changed from rage to sadness, her arms spread imploringly.

"Sarah dear, come back. Please. Please come back."

Sarah dashed for the gate and into the darkness, hearing her mother call "I have to tell you something, Sarah. Please come back."

Somehow, in the darkness, Sarah made her way to a friend's house and asked if she could stay the night. She had no idea where her father lived, and decided she would look for him in the morning.

"I told my mum where I was going," she said, after explaining that they'd had a row about nothing really, while Piggy goaded her mother to greater excesses of wounded pride and indignant anger than Sarah had ever experienced before. "It will give us both a chance to cool off."

Next morning, she began looking for her father, but no one in the village, and no one in the town, who might have known where he was, had any idea of his whereabouts. One or two family friends, people her mother hadn't seen for ages, looked at her in a puzzled way, but said nothing. Finally, after four days of looking, four days without success, she decided it was time to go home again. Her friend's family had been very kind, but she felt that she could stay in their home no longer. She was surprised that the police hadn't gone around the village trying to find her, knocking on doors, asking questions. That, she thought, was the measure of her mother's lack of interest in her. She wasn't looking forward to the coming confrontation.

She dawdled along the village street, turning off into the woods; the ground was squidgy from recent rain and her shoes were covered with mud, but she didn't care. She saw shadows moving among the trees, but she wasn't afraid because she'd seen them often. They were harmless. Maybe they were the woodland folk. The thought made her smile, it was a small smile, a fleeting smile, but it was real.

"I'm glad you're going back to mum," a man's voice said, a voice so soft it might have been nothing but a movement of air. "She's not perfect, but you need each other."

Sarah turned in a full circle. There was no one to be seen, but in the air was her father's fragrance, a scent of aftershave, toothpaste and cigars. For a moment she felt sad, then happiness washed over her and tears of happiness streamed from her eyes. Laughing, she came out of the woods and crossed the road. She saw her mother waiting at the door, smiling. Then, still laughing, she opened the garden gate.

Fire

Each morning when he awoke, Lynton got out of his bed, went to the en-suite bathroom, showered, brushed his teeth, flossed and shaved. He dried himself, dried his hair and applied a small amount of hair gel—enough to keep him looking smart throughout the day—and combed his hair. He sprayed deodorant beneath his arms and applied cologne lightly to his cheeks and neck. When he was satisfied that the morning ritual was completed as well as he could complete it, he returned to his bedroom and selected his clothes for the day. He liked coordinated colours, so to go with his dark blue business suit he chose a pale blue shirt, an un-patterned brown tie and dark blue socks; the colour of his underwear didn't bother him, although it was usually white.

When he was dressed to his satisfaction, he carefully folded his suit jacket over his left arm and went down to the kitchen. Since Jennifer had left him six months earlier, no aroma of cooking bacon greeted him, no smell of fresh coffee, no cheery good morning or kiss on the cheek. Sometimes he missed that.

He and Jennifer were still friends, but she had decided that living together didn't work for her. She told Lynton that he was too punctilious in his habits, too careful in his choice of words. She said there was nothing spontaneous about him and that meant there were no surprises in their relationship. She said that sometimes he annoyed her with his predictability. He argued that if that was so he would change, but he didn't change, and six weeks later they had the same conversation again—almost verbatim. When he returned from work that day, Jennifer had packed her things and left. There was no note.

For the first two or three weeks after Jennifer left, he felt more alone than he had for many years, but gradually his life had settled down again, and he convinced himself that the very things that had caused Jennifer to leave, his punctiliousness, his routines, were the things that had helped him get through their separation.

A month passed before he heard from Jennifer. His 'phone rang and when he answered it was her voice he heard. She was worried about him. She hoped he was alright. She hoped he was remembering to eat properly. Maybe they could have dinner together, not yet, but soon. They both refrained from asking the other if they were seeing anyone else. After that she called him at least once a week, but would always withhold her number and refuse to give an address.

As he waited for fresh coffee to splutter through the grind-and-brew machine he had bought, he crossed to the fireplace and took a photograph from the mantelpiece above. It was a picture of Jennifer of course, she was smiling and her auburn hair, though unmoving in the picture, danced around her face. He stared at the picture fondly, how he still longed for her presence, her touch, her soft, warm laughter. Then he kissed the picture and replaced it on its shelf above the fireplace.

Getting his dustpan and brush from the kitchen he bent over and carefully swept up the light grey ash and small curls of burnt paper that were on the hearth. That too had become a morning ritual. He had no idea where the ash came from, the fire was electric and nothing burned there except ersatz flames. In an unusually contemplative moment he wondered if his passion for Jennifer had somehow burst into physical form without him noticing, had burned for a moment and fallen as ash. But he knew this was a ridiculous notion.

His daily life was neither happy nor sad. He had friends, he had things to do and places to go—and he had his work. Days, weeks and months passed and he knew a kind of contentment, but always it was anticipating a call from Jennifer that gave him the most pleasure. After they'd spoken, after her voice was gone and the 'phone was replaced on its cradle, he always felt a sense of anti-climax, a bereftness that didn't pass away until he'd fallen asleep that night and awoken again the next morning—then he felt an emptiness that needed to be filled by his own busyness.

When he didn't hear from Jennifer for two weeks in succession, he began to worry. He worried for Jennifer, thinking that something might have happened to her, and he worried for himself because his routine was interrupted, and he disliked it intensely when that happened.

Two weeks became three and three became four, and he reasoned that Jennifer had found someone else. That was terrible for him, but he still had her photograph, he still hoped.

As he stood there, dustpan in hand, he picked up the photograph of Jennifer again, kissed it again, replaced it again. That was a break in his routine, and his actions annoyed him.

****

Another six months passed and Lynton became more and more obsessed with the small rituals that dominated his life. They were unimportant, he knew that. But he couldn't alter his habits. On the few occasions that he'd tried to do things differently, bad things happened; perhaps he spilled coffee on himself, or almost had an accident driving his car, or forgot to do something important at work and had to explain himself to his obnoxious manager. For these things he always blamed his breaks with routine, and the next day he returned to his punctilious ways and the world was alright again.

One morning, while he was eating the breakfast of muesli and Greek yoghourt that he always ate, he saw his photograph of Jennifer burst into flames. His first reaction was disbelief. This couldn't happen. It wasn't supposed happen. It wasn't part of his routine. By the time these thoughts had passed through his mind, the flames had gone and pale grey ash and small curls of burned paper were drifting down to the hearth. Only when he had finished his breakfast did he cross to the fireplace to look.

Although he'd already cleared the hearth of ash once that morning, as he always did, he went to the kitchen and returned with his dustpan and brush, then carefully swept up the ash.

It was not in him to be alarmed or surprised by what he had witnessed, but at least he thought he now knew where the ash in the hearth came from. Any explanation as to how the photograph caught fire each night and then was whole again next morning wasn't his concern. It was just something that happened. He disposed of the ash, replaced the dustpan and brush in the cupboard and was drying his hands after washing his breakfast dishes, when the doorbell rang. Another break with routine, and it bothered him.

****

A few minutes later, when the policeman had left, Lynton put on his jacket, locked the house door and went to work. He drove as he always did, but he was at least ten minutes late.

He thought about what the policeman had told him. He knew he would never see Jennifer again. Even her photograph had failed to reappear. He knew he would never hear her voice again as well. Those were things he had already accepted, even before the policeman's visit.

He thought he should feel sad that Jennifer had died in a house fire. He thought he should want to understand why it had taken more than five months to identify her remains. He thought he should want to know how the police had found out about his relationship with Jennifer. But those things were not a part of any one of his routines, and he let the thoughts drift away. He would miss the photograph of Jennifer though. That was a break with routine he would need to factor into his life.

Water

It wasn't so much that she was lonely, not in any real sense. She had plenty of friends in the town; they invited her out and visited often. They made sure that her life was full, just as good friends should. She spent very little time alone, and when she was alone she played music quite loudly, or turned the television on so that it drowned out the silence and it wasn't as if she were alone. Sooner or later Peter returned from work and the music or TV were turned down, or switched off, and she wasn't alone any more.

She would prepare their evening meal, the simple, wholesome food that Peter loved. They would talk and laugh. Sometimes, after dinner, they walked along their quiet street until they came to the pub on the corner. It was called The Waggoner's Arms, but there was no coat of arms on the swinging sign and the origins of the name were lost to time. Inside, they met people they knew and talked about unimportant things to an accompaniment of raucous laughter. Peter drank best bitter and sneered at anyone who ordered lager, a boys' drink he called it. She drank white wine spritzers. When the landlord called 'last orders' they dawdled back to their comfortable home, a home made from Peter's hard work and perspiration—and her own feminine skills. Then they would drink Ovaltine, or not—depending on their mood, and go to bed. It was a routine. It was their routine, and it suited them very well.

Each morning, except Saturdays and Sundays, they got up at around seven. She made breakfast, while Peter prepared himself for work. He was a teacher. He taught carpentry skills at a local college. After he left the house, after she watched him climb into their car and slam its door, after he reversed out into the street and drove away, always with a little tooting of the cars horn, she went back into the house. There, she cleared away the breakfast things as loud music played from the radio in the kitchen. She did the washing up, perfunctorily dusted and tidied their living room. When that was done, she went upstairs to the bedroom.

She sat on the edge of the bed and stared down at the small pool of water on the wood-laminate floor. It was always on her side of the bed, never on Peter's, so he always failed to notice it.

Every morning it was there, with one or two isolated drops trailing away to the bedroom door. The first time she had noticed the water it puzzled her, but she simply grabbed some Kleenex from the box on her bedside cabinet and wiped the spill away. By later in the day she had forgotten all about it. That's how it was for the first few weeks the water was there, but gradually she began to wonder where it came from. She never mentioned it to Peter. She knew he would worry about a leaking roof or a leaking pipe in the attic, even though there was no damage to the ceiling.

Months passed, and wiping away the water became just another part of her morning routine, but its routineness didn't stop her wondering. One day she decided to go to the library. There she used a computer to research spontaneous appearances of water. There were a few mentions of strange occurrences like the appearance of her water. There were reports, too, of statues crying and water flowing from ancient walls or solid rock. Without exception these manifestations were interpreted as signs from God. She didn't believe in god and so couldn't accept such explanations. Although she liked the idea of crying statues, they had no statues at home. When she left the library to meet a friend for lunch, she had, essentially, learned nothing.

The following morning, she was still thinking of a statue that cried, and tears were very much on her mind. As she sat on the edge of their bed, she leaned forward and dipped a finger into the water near her feet. She sniffed at her moist fingertip, but there was no odour that she could detect. Then she cautiously dabbed her finger onto her tongue, and instantly tasted the slight salinity of the water. To be certain, she repeated the experiment—and yes, there was a slight saltiness to the water.

Tears, she thought. I have tears beside my bed. She knew it was irrational. She knew it was impossible, unless… She let the thought tail off; it was getting uncomfortably close to the thing they never mentioned, the thing her friends never mentioned, a great sadness in her, in their lives, that they had successfully built an emotion-proof mental wall around.

Still she said nothing to Peter about the water.

Her life continued. She kept busy, she laughed a lot, she went out a lot, she joined a gymnasium where she made new friends. She was happy and contented with her life, or so she thought. Every now and then, however, her thoughts turned dark and the thing they never mentioned began to demolish the wall in her mind.

During a restless night's sleep, perhaps nine months after the water first appeared, she heard a sound that frightened her. It was a very soft sound, but when she strained her hearing to catch it, it was so mournful, so bereft of hope that it made her want to weep. After about ninety seconds, and with her eyes brimming with tears, she nudged Peter until he woke up.

"Do you hear that?" She asked, her voice barely able to hold back its sobs. "Do you hear that, Peter?"

Peter was silent for a moment.

"I hear nothing," he said.

"You don't hear that child crying?"

"It's probably just an insect outside."

"No," she said, "it's here, in this room."

"I can't hear anything except your voice. Let me sleep, please, please."

"I thought it might be..." she said.

"Don't start that again, we're over it. It does no good, no good at all, to dwell on what happened."

They both fell silent, and by and by sleep came to them. Even in the grip of tiredness, neither of them had actually mentioned the thing they never mentioned.

Next morning, Peter said nothing about their mild nocturnal altercation. She thought he had probably forgotten it already.

After he left the house, after she watched him climb into their car and slam its door, after he reversed out into the street and drove away, with a little tooting of the car's horn, she did the things she always did, like a good and dutiful wife. When she reached the bedroom she sat on the bed just as she always did, then she tasted the salt water on the floor as had become her habit. She began to cry.

She thought about their daughter. Emma had been six years old when she left the world. An illness without a name had taken her. She had died in a hospital bed.

"Thank you mummy," she had whispered with her last breath.

It had taken two years for them to get over the loss, two years for their child's death to become the thing they never mentioned.

She lost track of the time as she sat on the bed.

"Emma," she said over and over, "is that you darling. Are you here. Talk to me darling."

Outside the sun shone, the birds sang. She heard mail drop onto the doormat, she heard the telephone ring.

In their bedroom though, was only silence, in her was only pain and emptiness.

On the floor, by her feet, the little pool of water was fed by her own tears.

Lightning Source UK Ltd.
Milton Keynes UK
UKHW011320210223
417314UK00004BA/253